Megan recognized the dark-haired man now steppin̶̶̶̶̶̶̶̶̶ ̶̶̶̶̶̶̶̶̶̶̶̶̶̶̶̶̶̶̶̶̶̶̶̶̶̶̶̶s that crossed̶̶̶̶̶

Nick Ventura.

She heartily wi̶s̶̶̶̶̶̶̶̶ ̶̶̶̶̶̶̶̶̶̶̶̶̶̶̶̶̶̶̶̶̶̶̶̶̶̶̶ue man. And certainly wished that she hadn't ever slept with him.

Straightening her shoulders, she glared up at the brilliant blue sky before turning to face Nick, hopefully with a relatively normal expression on her face.

The smile he flashed was just as sexy as it had been that first time in Colbys Bar & Grill two and a half months ago.

Had she known then that falling for that appealing smile would land her in her current predicament, she wouldn't have gone near him with a ten-foot pole.

But as he got closer, she looked into his eyes.

She'd forgotten just how gray they were.

Ten-foot pole?

Who was she kidding?

* * *

RETURN TO THE DOUBLE C: Under the big, blue Wyoming sky, this family discovers true love

Dear Reader,

Megan Forrester is a strong, fiercely independent woman. She stands on her own two feet. She knows her own mind and isn't influenced by the opinions of those around her. Good things, yes?

Well, maybe not so much. Not when that streak of independence is so wide that it has become more like a weapon—against herself and others. When "independence" is the excuse to push others away because a) it is safer and b) it is safer.

Fortunately for Megan, there are men like Nick Ventura. Nick is a confident man and he can see beyond the surface to the inner Megan. To the strong and beautiful woman who is not only capable of competently steering her own ship, but the one who is simply afraid. Of disappointment. Of rejection. Of love.

The challenge for Nick is to help Megan see herself through *his* eyes. And to realize that real strength isn't necessarily measured by the ability to stand alone. Sometimes it is measured by the willingness to accept the one who wants to stand with you.

Allison

The Horse Trainer's Secret

ALLISON LEIGH

HARLEQUIN

SPECIAL
EDITION

If you purchased this book without a cover you should be aware
that this book is stolen property. It was reported as "unsold and
destroyed" to the publisher, and neither the author nor the
publisher has received any payment for this "stripped book."

HARLEQUIN®
SPECIAL EDITION™

Recycling programs
for this product may
not exist in your area.

ISBN-13: 978-1-335-40798-6

The Horse Trainer's Secret

Copyright © 2021 by Allison Lee Johnson

All rights reserved. No part of this book may be used or reproduced in
any manner whatsoever without written permission except in the case of
brief quotations embodied in critical articles and reviews.

This is a work of fiction. Names, characters, places and incidents
are either the product of the author's imagination or are used fictitiously.
Any resemblance to actual persons, living or dead, businesses,
companies, events or locales is entirely coincidental.

This edition published by arrangement with Harlequin Books S.A.

For questions and comments about the quality of this book,
please contact us at CustomerService@Harlequin.com.

Harlequin Enterprises ULC
22 Adelaide St. West, 40th Floor
Toronto, Ontario M5H 4E3, Canada
www.Harlequin.com

Printed in U.S.A.

Though her name is frequently on bestseller lists, **Allison Leigh**'s high point as a writer is hearing from readers that they laughed, cried or lost sleep while reading her books. She credits her family with great patience for the time she's parked at her computer, and for blessing her with the kind of love she wants her readers to share with the characters living in the pages of her books. Contact her at allisonleigh.com.

In loving memory of my aunt Janet.

Prologue

"It's agreed, then. We'll see you back here the middle of May."

Megan Forrester nodded at Jed Dalloway as everyone around the table clinked their frosty beer mugs together in a toast. "Middle of May," she agreed. "I'm looking forward to it."

Jed's wife, April, smiled broadly. "So are we! It's hard to believe that we've actually broken ground on our guest ranch."

"Believe it." Chance Michaels slid off his barstool as he fit the cap in place on the long tube containing his rolled-up architectural drawings. "Only now, this damn weather's got the ground frozen again."

The March weather was pretty miserable right now in Wyoming. And high up on Rambling Mountain, which overlooked the town of Weaver, it was even snowier. Once the guest ranch was built and open for business, that snow would be a major attraction for guests both far and near. But right now, it stood in the way of construction.

It also prevented Megan from making the several-hour drive back home to Angel River tonight.

"There's Nick." April abruptly set down her mug and waved her hand in the air. She glanced at Megan. "My cousin."

Megan didn't look up; she was busy refilling her mug. She figured she might as well take advantage of the fact that she wouldn't be driving home tonight.

It was a Friday night. Despite the inclement weather, Colbys Bar & Grill was crowded. Two guitarists and a drummer were crammed in one corner playing music that probably wouldn't land them a recording deal anytime soon, but they were good enough to have people dancing on one side of the bar, where the tables had been shoved aside. On the opposite side, every pool table was in use and the clacking of billiard balls was audible between one song and the next.

It was noisy. It was energetic. It was everything that, on occasion, Megan Forrester enjoyed. And on this occasion, she had something to celebrate. It wasn't every day when a woman like her was asked to design an equestrian center from the ground up.

"I'm gonna get on home before the wife hunts me down," Chance said, and Megan realized he'd already pulled on his coat. He tapped the cardboard tube lightly against the edge of the table. "Jed, I'll send you the plans for your cabin remodel this week, too," he promised before turning and making his way toward the door.

"Cabin remodel?"

April nodded and whipped out her cell phone, showing Megan a photo. "The view's spectacular, but you can see it needs a little updating," she joked. The picture showed an ancient, ramshackle cabin.

Megan peered at it a little more closely. "That's where the two of you *live*?" There were only a few tiny windows, and it looked in actual danger of sliding off the cliff where it was perched.

"It does have indoor plumbing," Jed interjected as a stranger in a cowboy hat grabbed the barstool Chance had just vacated.

"Mind if I take this?" The guy was already starting to slide it away, but a second stranger clamped his hand over the back of the chair.

"I do. Sorry, pal." His smile was white. He was tall and dark-haired. His eyes were gray. And they danced over April and Jed before landing on Megan's face.

Every female cell she possessed stood up and took notice as the man sat down in Chance's place.

The architect had been pleasant enough. Sixty-five, if he was a day, with thinning gray hair and a dulling gold wedding band on his finger. He'd seemed to know his stuff and Megan figured she could tolerate working with the guy for a couple months when she returned to Weaver in May. She'd work with almost anyone if it meant having the opportunity to design some stables and buy a lot of horses.

But that was business.

And this guy, with his broad shoulders and sexy grin, looked like anything but business. In fact, he looked like a long slow roll in the hay.

And it had been a very long time since Megan had rolled in any hay.

"Megan, this is my cousin—"

"I'm Nick," the man said before April could finish speaking. He shook Megan's hand, and the look in his eyes told her that he was taking notice of her in return. "And you are...?"

"Megan." From the corner of her eye, she saw April toss up her hands and shrug. But Megan was far more focused on the feel of Nick's thumb as he slowly rubbed the back of her hand.

"Want to dance, Megan?"

She was stuck in town for the night at the very least. She was celebrating. And now, a mouthwatering guy had practically dropped right in her lap.

She slipped off her barstool to stand in the very narrow bit of space between them. His jean-clad thigh felt solid and warm against her. "Dancing will do..." She slowly turned her hand in his and returned the subtle caress. His gray gaze sharpened, and she smiled slightly. "For a start."

Chapter One

May

*P*lease, please, please let me get through this without losing my lunch.

Megan sucked harder on the lemon drop in her mouth and wiped the perspiration from her forehead before she pushed open her pickup door and got out.

But the second her boots hit the muddy ground, her stomach churned even harder. Her knees actually felt weak and the urge to get back in the truck and turn tail was almost irresistible.

Instead, she clamped her hand over the top of her truck door until her palm hurt and clenched her back molars until her jaw ached.

Because, one way or another, she *would* get through this.

She was Megan Forrester, for cripes' sake. She made her own way in this world. She didn't do second thoughts. She didn't do regrets. She played the cards that life dealt her, and she didn't sit around boo-hooing if that hand happened to suck big-time.

But, oh, she seriously didn't want to puke all over the ground on her very first day on the job. It was bad enough she was sweating through the red silk blouse she'd worn for no reason other than to prove she *could* wear silk if she wanted to.

She squeezed the cold metal a little harder and swallowed several times, breathing deeply.

Her best friend, Rory—who'd given her the damn blouse last Christmas—would have laughed herself silly at the image of Megan now trying to find a little Zen. But then, Rory was the whole reason Megan was standing here on the side of Rambling Mountain on a Monday morning in the middle of May with her boots sinking into two inches of mud. If not for Gage Stanton—Rory's new husband—Megan wouldn't have been offered this job in the first place.

For a moment, she indulged in a good amount of mental grumbling at her friend, who was off on another whirlwind trip with Gage, checking out another piece of prime real estate to add to his portfolio.

Megan realized her nausea was finally fading, and she'd stopped sweating.

She looked down at the mud. Truth be told, she

was more comfortable with mud than she was with silk. Not surprising for a person who generally preferred horses to people.

Considering everything, she should have just stuck with her usual cotton shirt and worn denim jeans. It wasn't as if she was trying to impress anyone.

Was she?

The sound of another vehicle door slamming made her stiffen. She looked over her shoulder toward the SUV that had pulled up some distance behind her.

She recognized the vehicle, and the dark-haired man now stepping up onto the wood planks that bridged the muddy ground.

Nick Ventura.

She heartily wished she'd never laid eyes on him. And certainly wished that she had never slept with him.

She exhaled again, quickly chewing the lemon drop and swallowing it as she shut her truck door. Then, straightening her shoulders, she turned to face Nick, hopefully with a normal expression on her face.

He was carrying a long cardboard tube that he waved in greeting. His smile was just as sexy as the one he'd flashed that first time in Colbys Bar & Grill two and a half months ago.

Had she known then that falling for that smile would land her in her current predicament, she wouldn't have gone near him with a ten-foot pole.

The rough-hewn lumber rattled under his feet as

he drew abreast of her, close enough now that she could see the color of his eyes.

She'd forgotten just how gray they were.

His smile deepened when he finally stopped a few feet away from her.

"Good to see you, stranger."

Under other circumstances, Megan would have probably agreed. Instead, she gave him an intentionally cool smile. "Nick. How are you?"

"Better now that the rain's finally stopped." He spread his arms slightly and his eyes actually seemed to twinkle. "Guess all we needed was for you to move here from Angel River."

She squinted against the bright sunlight, which she knew had to be the *real* cause of that twinkle. "That's me. Weather Goddess," she drawled and walked two paces through the sucking mud to step onto the temporary boardwalk. "And I didn't move here. This is just a temporary deal, remember? I'll be heading back to Angel River in a couple months." She didn't stop next to him, but headed for the long trailer at the end of the boardwalk.

The trailer wasn't much to look at, but it served as the nerve center for the entire project that was underway on Rambling Mountain. It was the same trailer where she'd met with April, Jed and their architect before the bad weather had chased them off the mountain down to Colbys Bar & Grill back in March.

At the time, there had been no boardwalk. No construction vehicles, no foundations laid, no half-built anything. Just a whole lot of plans for the guest ranch on the edge of a pristine wilderness that was to become Wyoming's newest state park.

And Megan had been thrilled that Gage had requested her input about the equestrian facilities at his new guest ranch. Yeah, she was his new wife's best friend who happened to be the head wrangler at the Angel River guest ranch, but Gage hadn't achieved his level of success by indulging in sentimental choices. Regardless of her title at Angel River, she was just a horse trainer. Pure and simple. And she'd never in her wildest dreams expected the job offer of helping *design* the facilities on top of overseeing the acquisition of the horses for the new ranch.

Despite her fast pace, Nick somehow managed to beat her to the door of the trailer. He held it open for her, gesturing with the tube of architectural drawings. "Beauty first."

She rolled her eyes and ignored his widening smile as she walked through the narrow doorway.

Only once she'd stepped inside did it occur to her that she ought to have wiped off her muddy boots first.

Swearing under her breath, she started to back out, only to bump right against Nick. She froze again, this time swearing not so softly under her breath. "Mud," she grumbled and started scraping her heels against the rough edge of the wooden walkway.

He chuckled. "Only way to keep mud out of the trailer is to have everyone take off their boots before going inside. Won't ever happen. Fortunately, mud dries and dirt sweeps." He tapped her shoulder with the end of the tube. "Come on. I want to see what you think of our progress before the others get here."

He entered the trailer ahead of her, which was a good thing. It gave her a moment to practice that pointless Zen breathing. Not because she was nauseated again, but because she could still feel the imprint of his fingers against her waist.

Megan's grandmother would have told her this was what she deserved. That the universe served up justice in one way or another.

Nick wasn't even supposed to be *part* of the guest-ranch development. The fact that he was an architect had never even been mentioned in March. Admittedly, the two of them hadn't wasted a lot of time talking.

They'd danced. They'd left Colbys Bar & Grill.

They'd spent the night in the motel room she'd rented.

Megan figured there was one good use for most men, and that snowy night, Nick Ventura had delivered.

She'd only learned of his involvement with the guest ranch two weeks ago, when April told her that Chance Michaels had backed out of the deal and that her cousin was taking over the job.

Megan had learned a lot of things two weeks ago, and she was still reeling.

If she could have backed out of her agreement with Gage and his partners at that point, she would have.

But Angel River had already contracted a replacement to cover her absence at the guest ranch for the next two months. And Megan had already deposited Gage's check.

And, most of all, Rory would have had questions.

Questions that Megan wasn't ready to answer.

Not yet, anyway.

If she scraped her boots any longer against the sawn edge of the wood, she'd start wearing away the leather.

Swallowing a sigh, she went inside the trailer.

The floor was covered in ugly gray tile. The perimeter was lined with utilitarian metal desks and shelves, while the walls were covered with calendars, schedules and drawings.

She was very aware of Nick's gaze as he uncapped his cardboard tube. Rather than face him, she made a point of studying the nearest drawing on the wall. It was an artist's rendering of the finished lodge. It made Angel River—which wasn't exactly tiny—look like a fishing camp. And it was only vaguely reminiscent of the drawing that Chance Michaels had sent to her after their meeting all those weeks ago.

"How've you been?"

"Good." She tapped the indecipherable signature at the corner of the drawing. "This is a lot more advanced than the drawing Chance Michaels gave me."

"A lot can happen in a couple months."

She managed not to react.

"Take a look." He unrolled the thick sheaf of papers on a desk and anchored the curling edges with a stapler on one side and a broken brick on the other. "Gage forwarded your latest comments on Chance's design to me, but I didn't have an opportunity to work some of them into the revised design until this week." He swept his palm flat across the blue-tinged paper.

He had long fingers. Square-tipped. Nails cut short and neat.

The way he'd used those fingers—

She curled her own fingers into her palms, cutting off the memory.

She leaned in to look at the drawings, bringing her closer to Nick. "*Some* of them?" She was irritated that she couldn't ignore the solid warmth of his body, and it sounded in her voice. "You left out the most important change of all. The stable is exactly the same size as it used to be."

"We can't expand the stable without relocating it."

She straightened again and pushed her fingers into her back pockets, edging away from him. The man radiated heat like a stovepipe. "So relocate it."

"Things don't happen just like that." He snapped his fingers.

"Where Gage Stanton is concerned, that's not true. When this all started out, it was just supposed to be a guest ranch. A small one. Two months later and it's basically a full-blown resort. Which is why I told Chance Michaels the horse barn had to be expanded, too. Not only does it need to house twice as many horses, but twice as much tack and feed and everything else."

Nick looked amused. "April and Jed are the ones overseeing this particular project. Gage and Stanton Development are sitting in the back seat on this one."

She barely managed not to snort. She knew from Rory that Gage had personal reasons for keeping his direct involvement in Weaver to a minimum. That he was intent on keeping his distance from a grandmother who didn't even know he existed. She figured that was why he was letting someone else do the driving. Still, if it hadn't been for him, Megan wouldn't be part of the project at all.

And right now, she wasn't entirely grateful.

"Considering everything," Nick said, "they're keeping things here pretty low-key. They're not trying to turn Weaver into the next Aspen or even the next Angel River."

Even Gage Stanton's golden touch couldn't create another Aspen out of Weaver, Wyoming. But another Angel River? "Have you ever *been* to Angel River?" The guest ranch was located near the Wyoming/ Montana border. The nearest town, Wymon, made Weaver look like a sprawling metropolis.

"No, but Gage had a lot to say about it."

She could well imagine that, considering he'd met Rory there. "Well, whatever, just based on the size of the operation, if there isn't a bigger stable, then you'll need two of them. Otherwise there won't be space for the number of horses a place this size will require. A guest ranch isn't a guest ranch without a good string of horses. And a good string of horses requires proper stabling."

"A second barn isn't in the plans, either."

On any other day, she would have been more than happy to argue the point. But with her stomach still feeling dicey, she merely shrugged. "The plans are wrong, then."

He turned and leaned his hip against the desk, crossing his arms over his chest. "You look nice in red."

She pressed her lips together. "What's that got to do with the stable?"

His gray eyes held hers despite her intense desire to look away. "Nothing." He waited a beat. "Why didn't you call me back?"

Her breath evaporated inside her lungs. "Back?"

"After the morning you disappeared from Weaver, I left you a couple messages at Angel River."

Three messages. He'd left three of them over the course of a month and Rory's dad had delivered each one himself. But after that, they'd stopped, and she'd been relieved. An occasional one-night stand was her style. A guy who called and called and called was not. "I don't think this is the place to talk about that."

He leaned forward, dropping his voice conspiratorially. "That's why you shouldn't have ignored the messages I left for you."

"I didn't ignore them."

"You *chose* not to answer them. Same thing."

She finally managed to drag her gaze free of his. "Depends on your point of view." They hadn't closed the trailer door and she stuck her head out, looking at the framed-in building straight ahead. It would be the main lodge when it was finished, its multiple stories built straight into the steep side of the magnificent mountain.

"I'm surprised that April and Jed aren't here yet." She glanced at the plain watch strapped around her wrist. "Your cousin was the one who called this meeting."

"They'll be here." Nick braced his hands on the doorjamb on either side of her to look out also, and he might as well have been touching her. She was tall, but he was taller, and she could feel his words stirring the hair at her temple.

She didn't want to think about the other stirrings he caused.

That was what had landed her in this state in the first place. Well, that and her own impetuous decisions. She couldn't very well pretend she hadn't been a more-than-willing participant.

"They're still living in Otis's cabin up on the Rad," he said, "so it's not like they have to drive up the mountain for the meeting."

She glanced beyond the lodge, where she knew the small, ancient cabin was located. The only thing she'd seen of it had been the photo that April had shown her. But since then, April had regaled her with the whole story of how Jed had more or less inherited the Rambling Rad Ranch from an old guy named Otis Lambert. The ranch wasn't much to speak of in terms of cattle. But when it came to the land it encompassed on Rambling Mountain? It was immense. As for the rest of the mountain that wasn't part of the Rad, Lambert had deeded it to the State of Wyoming, which had then declared it a new state park. That had made the adjacent Rambling Rad far more valuable in terms of tourism than it had ever been as a cattle ranch.

Thus, Megan assumed, the decision to build a guest ranch.

"Have you taken over the designs for rebuilding their cabin, too?"

"My father and I are working on it together." Nick's right hand moved from the doorjamb to settle on her shoulder. Lightly. Naturally.

As if he had a right.

It didn't matter that his touch set off a delighted ripple. Megan shifted slightly, hoping that he'd move away, but he didn't. She stepped forward, out of the doorway altogether, until his hand fell away. Then she turned around to face him.

He didn't even bother hiding his smile, as if he knew exactly how consternated she felt.

"Look," she said firmly, "what happened between us was just a one-time thing. One and done," she added for emphasis. "Got it?"

He didn't look at all chastened, though.

And dammit, there was that twinkle in his eye

again. The sun wasn't shining in through the doorway, so that didn't explain it this time.

"I'll agree that it was a one-*night* thing," he said. "But hardly one and done. If you hadn't snuck out of the motel room when I was still sleeping, it could've been three and four—"

She shot up a warning hand, but he broke off, anyway, looking past her to where April and Jed were approaching from the direction of the construction site.

He stepped around Megan and out the door. "Morning! I was about to send out a search party for the two of you."

"Blame Jed," April said cheerfully. Her long red ponytail was blowing in the breeze as she practically skipped along the wooden walkway with Jed and a huge, shaggy, wolfish-looking gray dog trailing behind her. "He just *had* to have waffles for breakfast this morning."

"And you didn't bring me any?" Nick spread his hands. "And here I thought I was your favorite cousin."

Given what Megan knew from April's chatter over the last few months, the other woman had more cousins than Carter had pills. First cousins. Second cousins. Whatever cousins.

In the family department, Megan only had her grandmother, Birdie.

April gave Nick a smacking kiss on the cheek before brushing right past him to hug Megan. "I'm *so* excited you're finally here! This is going to be so much fun, all of us working together." Without waiting for a response, she turned on the heel of her bright orange rubber boot and spread her arms wide, encompassing the construction site. "Isn't it amazing what's already been accomplished?"

"Gotta make hay while the sun shines," Jed said. "So far, it's been a mild spring, but you never know around here."

April bounced on her toes. "Want a tour?"

Her enthusiasm was hard to resist. And anything that interrupted Nick from going on about the night he and Megan had spent together was okay with her. She didn't usually consider herself a coward, but for now, avoiding the subject was the best approach. "Definitely."

"Hold on." Before she could take a step, Nick disappeared into the trailer and returned with an armful of hard hats. "Nobody allowed in the construction zone without one." He handed two to his cousin and her husband, then dropped a third on top of Megan's head. It fell over her eyes and he pulled it right back off, made a few adjustments and set it back in place. Then he nodded with satisfaction and they all headed toward the skeletal framework of the main lodge.

Megan wouldn't be working on the lodge itself, but she couldn't help being fascinated as they made their way through the structure. It was easy to visualize the completed building thanks to Nick's vivid descriptions and the amazing artist's rendering that had been hanging in the construction trailer.

She tried to imagine taking the same tour with Chance Michaels and being this excited, but couldn't.

When they reached the part of the lodge that would eventually cantilever out beyond the mountainside, Megan propped her arms on a crossbeam of lumber and looked down. The breeze was stiffer here, blowing her hair around beneath her hard hat, and she wished she'd worn it in a ponytail, like usual. She dragged it out of her eyes for the umpteenth time as she leaned forward a little to peer down at the jagged, rocky landscape. "So where does the state park actually start?"

April came up next to her and pointed. "Just a little above Lambert Lake." Her arm swept to the right. "Extends all the way down to the highway. The highway department's been working on grading an access road, but lack of a road hasn't stopped people from already starting to come to the mountain. Can't blame their curiosity, considering the land has always been private property."

Far below, Megan could see the whitish-blue glimmer of water nearly obscured by steep outcroppings of rocks and tall evergreen trees. When she turned her head, thanks to the fact that the structure around them possessed no solid walls yet, she was able to look upward toward the mountain summit. "A lot of it is still private property, isn't it? Do you and Jed own all the rest?" She'd never thought about a mountain being owned by anyone, but supposed it was no different than any other piece of property.

"We own it along with Gage," April said with a wry laugh. "Jed's still going to run the Rad. It'll still be a real cattle ranch, and then any of the guests who want that traditional 'ranch' experience can work the cattle with him. Whatever that entails."

Megan couldn't hide her amusement. "I'm guessing you don't work the ranch with him."

"Oh, I love horses and all that. I can work a roundup. But inoculations and castrations and branding?" Her eyes were filled with mirth. "Not on my particular top-ten list of things to do."

She looked over to where her husband and Nick seemed thick in discussion. The gray dog had disappeared somewhere along the way. "There's not a lot of cattle—Otis's spread was small in comparison to most around here—but the ranch is still important to Jed because it was important to Otis. But Jed also feels pretty strongly that the mountain shouldn't be off-limits to the public the way it's been for generations. This way, we have the best of both worlds."

"And making a profit in the process," Megan added dryly.

April laughed. "Well, there's that, too. Gage wouldn't be involved otherwise. I used to work for him. I was scoping out the situation on Rambling Mountain for Stanton Development when I met Jed, so I am *well* aware of Gage's business sense." She shook her head. "I'm still stunned that he turned out to be as human as the rest of us and fell for Rory. Delighted," she emphasized, "but stunned."

Megan looked over at Nick and Jed to see they'd hopped up onto a wooden beam easily six feet off the ground. Both men had dark hair. Nick was slightly taller. Jed looked slightly rougher. But they both seemed perfectly at ease as they walked along the beam.

Megan's stomach rolled a little and she exhaled carefully, turning again to look back down to the lake.

The landscape really was stunning. "Where's the ski run going to be?" She knew they were aiming to have the place open for business well before the Christmas holidays.

April pointed toward the slopes on their right. "There will be two to start, but in time there could be more. If things go well here and we can figure out how to actually get it built, there could be a smaller winter resort up at the summit with at least another three runs."

A summit that Megan couldn't even properly see because of the clouds ringing it. "The only skiing we have at Angel River is cross-country."

"You like to ski?"

Megan shrugged. "I prefer horses to most everything," she said truthfully. "Including people."

"But you deal with people all the time at Angel River, don't you? Organizing all the activities?"

"Taking a bunch of guests on daily trail rides or teaching 'em how to get on a horse for the first time is easy. Making sure they're having fun during the times when their butts aren't in a saddle is a small price to pay for getting to be around the horses." From the corner of her eye, she saw Nick nimbly hop down from the beam.

April chuckled. "I have a fair number of family members who think like you—horses, horses, horses." She moved over to where Jed had jumped down after Nick. "Including this one here." She patted her husband's chest and followed up with a kiss on his jaw.

"What's that for?"

"Just because you're cute."

"Think we know which one of us is cuter," he replied as his arms surrounded her.

"Come on." Nick touched Megan's elbow, making her jump. "Once they get going, they're likely to keep at it for a long while."

"I think he sounds jealous," April said to Jed.

Megan quickly moved away from Nick. She couldn't help but remember that night in March. When it came to "keeping at it," there wasn't any reason for Nick to feel jealous.

And now she was pregnant with his baby.

Which was something she had no intention of admitting.

Not yet, at least.

As far as she was concerned, what happened with her body was her business. And when she did tell him, like everything else in her life, it would be on her terms.

Without looking at him, she retraced their steps back to the trailer. "The tour was nice," she said briskly. "But about the stable..."

Chapter Two

"So how'd it go this morning with your horse trainer?"

Nick set his briefcase on the glass table and looked at Vivian Templeton. Even at home on a normal Monday in May, Vivian was dressed in a two-piece designer suit, complete with pearls at her neck and diamonds at her wrists. More often than not, the diminutive, white-haired woman was demanding and a general pain in his neck. But despite all that, she was one of his favorite people. Which was why, when he'd already finished designing the public library that she'd been determined to see built in Weaver, he'd agreed to work on her newest pet project even though his plate was already overflowing, thanks to having to take over nearly all of Chance Michaels's projects.

Not that he was complaining about the Rambling Mountain job. That involved a silver lining he couldn't resist.

"Megan Forrester isn't my horse trainer." He pulled out a pen and a yellow pad of paper from his briefcase, sat down on the cushioned bench opposite Vivian and pushed the enormous green leaf from the plant behind him away from his head. Meetings with Vivian were often conducted in her conservatory— the fancy word for her overgrown indoor tropical garden that by all reasoning should have failed to grow at all here in the heart of Wyoming.

"You want her to be."

He ignored that remark and flipped through his notes on the yellow pad, but Megan's image floated in his mind, making it difficult to concentrate on his chicken scratchings. For a month after she'd left Weaver, he'd tried to reach her at the guest ranch where she worked. He'd had no other means to contact her.

He hadn't given up when she'd refused to return his calls. He'd just been busy. And he'd known she'd be returning in a few months' time, anyway.

Nick Ventura was nothing if not a patient guy and Megan would now be staying in Weaver for weeks.

He clicked his pen a few times as if that would help get the tall, blue-eyed blonde off his mind. "I never should have told you about her."

"Ah, but you did." Vivian set her china cup on a saucer; it was just as likely to be filled with bourbon as with tea. The diamond rings on her fingers glinted in the sunlight angling through the tall windows. "And no backsies, as they say."

He couldn't help but laugh even as he glanced through the windows where Rambling Mountain stood tall and picturesque in the distance. "Let me guess. That's one of Delia's terms."

"What's one of my terms?" Vivian's granddaughter, Delia Templeton, sauntered into the conservatory, sucking some green concoction through a straw.

"Backsies," Vivian answered, sighing when Delia propped her hip on the scrolled iron arm of Vivian's chair. "Delia, dear, there are several other perfectly adequate and unoccupied chairs in here."

Delia's eyes were dancing as they met Nick's, but before she could take the narrow space next to him on the cushioned bench, he dropped his legal pad there and busied himself hunting through his briefcase for something.

Anything.

Because it had been obvious to him for a while now that Vivian's granddaughter had her eye on him.

His searching fingers sank into something soft shoved deep in one corner.

He didn't need to draw it out to know what it was.

The black knit stocking cap bearing the white Angel River logo that Megan had been wearing when she led the way to her motel room that memorable March night.

It was the only thing she'd left behind when she snuck out early the next morning.

"And what sort of thing do you want to take back?" Delia wasn't the least deterred by his legal pad. She just moved it out of the way and sank down beside him, then proceeded to page through his notes as if she had every right to do so.

He left the knit cap where it was, deep in the corner of his case, then lifted the pad out of Delia's hands and away from her nosy eyes.

It wasn't as though she didn't know most everything that Vivian was involved in since she was her grandmother's personal assistant. But his pad contained all his notes from the meeting that morning up on the mountain, which—while not exactly secret—weren't any of Delia's business, either.

She'd learned a lot in the way of discretion since Vivian had taken her under her wing, but Nick could still remember Delia from the days before Vivian had moved to Weaver.

Delia had always been good-natured and funny. But she would probably never get over her tendency to say nearly everything and anything that popped into her brunette head.

And now she made no secret of the fact that she'd been reading his scratchings. "Who's Megan?"

As was his usual habit, he'd headed the page with the date and time of his meeting and the names of those present.

"The horse trainer who's working with Jed and

April Dalloway," Vivian replied, returning the look he gave her with a bland one of her own. "Have you finished discussing the library's grand-opening menu with Montrose?"

Delia waved her hand, looking unconcerned. "The grand opening is almost two months away. There's oodles of time yet. Besides, Montrose is wallowing in one of his hissy fits."

"I do not—" the man himself had entered the conservatory bearing a silver tea tray "—have *hissy* fits." Vivian's high-maintenance chef was tall, bald as a cue ball and dressed in a black suit with a white cravat. She'd brought him with her when she'd moved to Wyoming from Pittsburgh and he was as unlikely a sight in Weaver as her tropical-plant-filled conservatory. He moved slowly, as if doing so somehow imparted how important his role there was. He set down the tray and placed an empty cup and saucer in front of Nick, then filled it with brown liquid that steamed from the silver pot before refilling Vivian's cup.

So she was drinking tea, Nick thought. At least this time.

He waited, trying not to show his impatience, as the man put a small plate of tiny sandwiches on the glass between the cups and saucers, followed by two small gold-rimmed plates and two perfectly folded linen napkins. Then, with his tray tucked beneath his arm, he straightened.

"What about me, Montrose?"

The man looked down his hooked nose at Delia,

and at the green goop in her crystal glass. "When the gardener finishes mowing the lawns, I'll be sure to mix you up more grass." He turned on the heel of one of his highly polished dress shoes and departed the sunroom as ceremoniously as he'd entered.

Delia sucked noisily through her straw in response.

"Please stop antagonizing Montrose," Vivian chided. "That's my job."

Delia just grinned and swung her foot, where a sparkling red flip-flop dangled from her toes.

"Help yourself, Nick, dear." Vivian waved a finger at the refreshments. "I know how you love Earl Grey tea."

He hated the stuff and had worked with her for a full year on the library project before finally admitting it.

Which was when she'd divulged the fact that her teacup didn't always contain tea.

He ignored the cup but did grab a handful of sandwiches. Combined, they didn't equal even one full sandwich, but he hadn't taken time to eat lunch after leaving Megan in the construction trailer on the mountain and he was starving.

Besides which, affected mannerisms or not, Montrose was a helluva cook. Nick didn't know what was in the little sandwiches and didn't much care. They were delicious.

He swiped his mouth with the napkin and flipped to a fresh page in his pad. "Okay. I've reviewed all the reports on the Gold Creek property, and everything

looks good. Most importantly, there's no asbestos is-
sues, so we won't have to deal with that when we start
gutting the place." He popped two more sandwiches
in his mouth and ignored the way Delia's shoulder
bumped his every time she swung her foot.

"And you have the presentation ready for the town
council?"

"Almost." The council was meeting in a few days.
"It'll be ready, though."

"I don't want any reason for them to shoot me
down."

"No reason why they would," he said confidently.

Her lips thinned. "Depends on the mood Squire
Clay is in," she said. "He's the newest member on the
council but all the rest fall into line behind whatever
he says. Have you sounded out the old man about
my plans?"

Nick gave a wry laugh. "Nobody sounds out
Squire."

"You're family."

"We're family by marriage, and it didn't influence him where the library plans were concerned, if
you'll remember."

"He came around on the library," Delia said.
"Maybe he won't put up any argument about turning that old commercial building into something use-
ful, like an athletic center."

"He'll put up an argument just because he still
hates me for things that happened long before even
your parents were born." Vivian brushed nonexistent

lint from her sleeve. "You'd think he'd have other things to focus on these days."

Nick figured that was a reference to the fact that Squire and his wife had been separated for the better part of a year. And as much as he liked Vivian, he wasn't going to get into a conversation about *that*. Not when his own stepmother was Gloria Clay's granddaughter.

He flipped through the files in his oversize case again and pulled out a folded drawing that he handed to Vivian. "Here's the rendering that you wanted."

She set the thick paper on her knees. "Delia, dear. My reading glasses are up in my office. Would you mind getting them?"

To her credit, Delia didn't complain about the request. She left the room, her flip-flops making a loud slapping sound, and Nick exhaled slightly, spreading his work again on the seat beside him since the small glass table had no room left.

Then Vivian unfolded the drawing and slipped a pair of glasses out of her pocket. "Don't worry, Nick. My granddaughter will stay busy for at least a half hour trying to find these." She put on the glasses and peered at the sketch.

"I wasn't worried."

"You're very kind not to encourage her."

He grimaced. "Vivian."

"I'm old, dear. Not blind. In time, Delia's interests will land elsewhere. You could help hurry her along if you'd just admit you've been pining for the horse trainer from Angel River for two months now."

He nearly choked on the sandwich he'd just put in his mouth. He took a swallow of the hot tea, which tasted like dirt, and wiped his mouth again. "I haven't been pining." He tossed aside the napkin again. "So, back to the athletic center. If we get the plans approved quickly enough, I'm estimating that you'll be able to open for business by the beginning of the year."

She looked at him above the rims of her narrow reading glasses. "I was hoping for sooner."

"You're always hoping for sooner, Vivian."

"Yes, well, at this stage of my life I've learned to plan in terms of months versus years." She looked back at his pen-and-ink drawing. "I've told you before, Nick, that if you ever want to switch careers, I have an entire wing upstairs where I'd be happy to hang your artwork."

"It's a nice offer, but I'll stick with architecture, thanks."

"I'm sure your father is pleased. He must be happy that you've joined his firm."

"Most of the time." He smiled. "Unless we're arguing over who has the privilege of working with you on your latest brainstorm."

Vivian chuckled. "Or who has the displeasure of being stuck with me."

"I'm not touching that one," he said, waving off

the sketch when she refolded it and started to hand it to him. "Keep it."

She set it back down on her lap. "All kidding aside, I do appreciate you indulging me when it comes to our little meetings. I know we could have dealt with this with a phone call, but I prefer conducting business in person. I'm old-fashioned, I'm afraid."

"Vivian, even if you weren't paying the bills, I'd be happy to meet with you in person." He winked as he gestured at the empty plates. "Montrose has the best food."

She smiled and stood, and he knew from experience that their meeting was concluded. He dumped his things back in his case and rose to shake her hand. Gently, because the woman did look frailer than her demeanor indicated. "Next week, same time?"

"If you don't mind."

Even if he had, he wouldn't have said so and it had nothing to do with the hefty retainer fees she'd paid into the coffers of Ventura & Ventura Architects. He might have started out frustrated as all hell with the woman over her impossibly lofty plans for the library, but as he'd gotten to know her, he'd grown to respect her opinions even when he didn't necessarily agree with them. Now he could say that he genuinely liked the eccentric woman.

And he appreciated the brevity of the meeting if it meant he could escape without another encounter with her granddaughter.

After he left Vivian's mansion, he picked up a

normal-size turkey sandwich at Ruby's Diner in town, sliding in just in time before they closed for the afternoon, and then returned to his office. He was sitting at his drafting table, halfway through eating the sandwich, when his father walked in.

Beckett Ventura walked over and studied the plans spread out in front of Nick. "Heard your horse trainer's all checked in at the Cozy Night. Arrived late yesterday."

"She's not my horse trainer." How many times did he have to say it? "And glad to know the Weaver hotline is as active as ever." He rotated on his seat, looking from the prints to the two computer screens that displayed the same plans. He moved a few lines, corrected a few angles, then sighed and undid the changes. "I don't know why she needs such a big damn barn." He tossed down his pencil and stretched.

Beck looked amused. "One thing I've learned since I came to Weaver is that barns gotta be big whether they're housing equipment or livestock."

"No kidding," Nick muttered. He hadn't grown up here in Weaver. When his mom died while he'd been off at college, his dad had closed his thriving firm, sold off their family home in Denver and hidden himself away in the dinky town of Weaver. He'd even given up architecture altogether until he'd fallen for Lucy Buchanan. In time, Beck started a new firm. One that focused more on farmhouses than the skyscrapers he'd previously been known for.

When Nick had graduated from Princeton with

his own degree, he hadn't really envisioned setting up shop with his dad. But after knocking around the world for a few years working on the sorts of projects he'd thought he'd wanted to do, he'd ended up right back in Weaver, where he could run his *own* projects.

"The problem with this barn—" he turned back to the plans on his drafting table "—is that it was scaled to serve a simple dude ranch."

"Nothing about Rambling Mountain has ever been simple, even when Otis Lambert was alive."

Nick didn't have to close his eyes to summon a vision of Megan Forrester wearing brilliant red, her dark blond hair streaming in the wind beneath a bright yellow hard hat.

Things still weren't simple, that's for sure.

"You'll figure out a solution for the barn. Meanwhile, Lucy's fixing meat loaf tonight. You want to come for supper?"

He'd started shaking his head even before his dad finished speaking. "You know I love my stepmother, but I'll pass."

Beck chuckled. "She's using your grandpa's recipe."

Stan Ventura had become quite a cook when he'd started helping out with Nick's little sister, who'd been only three when their mom died. "I'm sure that helps," Nick allowed because, when it came to Lucy's cooking, most anything would help, "but I'll still pass. Tell her I've got a late meeting."

"Do you?"

He thought about Megan at the Cozy Night. None of the rooms there were equipped with actual kitchens. Maybe she'd be content with a cup of soup heated up in a microwave. And maybe not.

"I hope to," he said. He figured he could wrangle some of her time, particularly if he brought up the subject of the stable. She'd argued with him for damn near an hour before he'd had to come down off the mountain for his meeting with Vivian.

As if his father could read his mind, Beck smiled. "Good luck with that." Then he left Nick's office.

He could hear his dad talking with Gina, the office manager, and then the distinctive creak of the front door as he left.

Nick gave up the pretense of studying his plans and opened his briefcase. He pulled out the knitted beanie and flattened it against his drafting table. "One and done, my foot," he said under his breath.

Then he turned back to his computer screens again. He moved a few lines. Tweaked a few angles.

Because if Megan wanted a bigger barn, he was going to find a way to give it to her.

He just hadn't been inclined to admit that to her in light of her attitude today.

Their one night together had ended abruptly with the close of a motel-room door shortly after dawn. But he knew that the incendiary heat that had burned between them hadn't gone cold in the two and a half months since. He'd seen it in her eyes this morning every time she looked his way and thought he wasn't paying attention.

Patience, Nick. You'll get so much further if you're patient.

The words had practically been his mother's mantra while he was a kid, whether she was teaching him how to coax a scared cat out of a tree, or how to keep control of his own temper. Even though she'd died a decade ago, they were still a frequent refrain in Nick's head.

He continued working until Gina yelled that she was heading out for the day, then he packed up his things and followed her out.

He ran by his place—one of the new condos located across town—where he dumped off his briefcase, showered and shaved in record time, and headed out again, back across town to the Cozy Night.

He found out from the clerk in the office what room Megan was staying in—which wasn't exactly a stellar example of honoring the guests' privacy—and drove to the end of the building.

She was sitting in the salmon-colored metal chair outside her room, her long legs extended and crossed at the ankles. The ends of her thick hair drifted slightly in the breeze and she was holding a paper cup.

He knew the second she recognized his SUV pulling into the empty spot next to her mud-spattered pickup because she exploded out of the chair like a racehorse from the gate and disappeared inside the room.

Not exactly an auspicious start.

He finished parking and exhaled as he approached the closed door. The number on the door—22—was just as askew now as it had been in March. He'd always known the universe had a quirky sense of humor.

Seemed perfectly fitting that she was in the same damn room now.

He straightened the number and knocked.

Considering the way she had bolted inside, he was surprised at how quickly she opened the door.

She'd replaced the red blouse from that morning with a blue plaid shirt that snapped down the front. The muddy cowboy boots were gone, too, leaving her feet bare. But the blue jeans that emphasized her narrow hips and long, long legs were the same.

"I'm not inviting you in." Her voice was blunt, almost to the point of being pugnacious.

"Didn't expect you to," he countered mildly. "Doesn't mean I can't invite you out. Have you had dinner?"

Her lips thinned. "I told you. One and—"

"Done. Yeah. Got it." It was easy to see around her into the room.

There were two medium-size suitcases sitting open on one of the beds. She hadn't unpacked; the closet was still empty. Next to the closet was a small counter with a microwave on top and a dinky fridge beneath it. On the counter was a lone, disposable coffee cup and the cheap basket that he knew would contain instant coffee, a tea bag and a cup of ramen noodle soup.

"I'm not talking about a date," he told her. "I'm talking about dinner."

She rolled her eyes and leaned her shoulder against the doorjamb. "What for? You won't change my mind." Her gaze focused somewhere over his shoulder. "The night we had was fun and all, but that moment has passed."

If she'd met his eyes when she said it, he'd have believed her. And he'd have filed away his own interest whether he wanted to or not.

But she hadn't met his eyes.

"And, anyway—" she shifted again "—I don't mix business and pleasure."

He hid a smile. "If you don't want to know where the horse barn's going to be relocated, it's no sweat to me." He turned and took a step past the salmon chair.

"Is it bigger?"

He paused and turned back around. "No reason to move it if it wasn't."

Her eyes narrowed. "You could just tell me now."

He shrugged. "True. But I'm hungry."

She frowned. "Maybe I'm not."

He just waited.

After a full minute, she made an annoyed sound. Her shoulders came down and she flopped her hands. "Fine. But *just* dinner."

He smiled. "Just dinner."

It was a good enough place to start.

* * *

Rather than take Megan to Colbys Bar & Grill, which would have been Nick's first choice if he weren't avoiding reminders of that night in March, he took her to a pizza joint not far from his condo.

Pizza Bella had good food. He didn't know what the secret was with their crust, but it was better than most. And they had even better beer.

It was just a happy coincidence that the booths provided an undeniable sense of intimacy.

No matter how hard Megan tried to keep her long legs from knocking against his beneath the small table, she couldn't, and when she swore under her breath for the third time before they'd even gotten past their bruschetta appetizer, Nick was unable to hold back a laugh.

"Do you *ever* relax?"

She had refused the beer and was white-knuckling a tall glass of lemonade. "I don't know what you mean."

He shook his head. "At the risk of having you take my head off for the observation, you weren't this up-tight before."

"I am not uptight."

"Right. Squeeze that glass any harder and it might break in two." He leaned his forearms on the table. "Look, Megan. Seriously. You want to pretend that night between us didn't happen, then that's what we'll do. I'm a grown man. I can pretend there's no attraction between us." But he wasn't going to lie outright and say there was none.

She started to open her mouth and he lifted his fingers. "Just hear me out."

She clamped her lips together again.

"You're going to be here in Weaver for at least the next couple months—"

"At *least*?" Her eyes widened with obvious alarm. "At most, you mean. I'm supposed to be back at Angel River in July."

He decided that now probably wasn't the best time to explain the realities of construction and how the law of averages meant that timelines and budgets almost always ran over.

"Regardless, we're going to be working together on the equestrian facilities. That's the whole reason you're here." He sat back. "It'll be a lot easier if you just trust that I'm not going to try to get you into bed every time you turn around." It wasn't entirely true. He'd be more than happy to get her back into bed. But he did have a job to do. And he had respect for a woman's boundaries.

She quirked an eyebrow. "I don't think you're trying to get me into bed every time I turn around." She sounded resentful.

"All right, then." He spread his hands. "Gage Stanton wanted you involved here because he trusts your expertise. And the guy's never wrong. Combine your expertise with mine and we'll create something—"

She suddenly pushed away from the table. "Sorry," she mumbled, "I'll be right back."

Frowning, he watched her hurry out of the dining room, narrowly avoiding the teenage server bringing their pizzas—the heart-attack special for Nick and the cheese-and-basil one for her.

"She comin' back?" The kid placed the pizzas and a stack of extra napkins on the table.

"Yeah."

The teenager looked skeptical. "There's a window in the ladies' bathroom, dude. Yesterday, some guy's date climbed out of it."

"She'll come back," Nick said with a lot more confidence than he suddenly felt.

"Well, if she doesn't—" the server gestured at the cheese-and-basil pizza "—I can wrap that whole thing up for you to go."

"She'll be back," he repeated flatly. Then he picked up his beer and tried not to think about the way she'd snuck out of her own motel room while he'd slept.

Chapter Three

Megan stared at her reflection in the narrow mirror next to the curtained window and pinched her cheeks until they no longer looked so pale.

How was she going to explain any of this to Nick without actually explaining any of this?

The locked door behind her rattled and she quickly turned on the water in the sink.

"Mommy, I gotta *go*," a young voice said, and Megan's shoulders sagged. She couldn't hide out in the ladies' room forever even if she wanted to.

When had she turned into such a coward?

She washed her hands, turned off the water and unlocked the door to find a little girl and her mom standing just outside. The girl was doing the pee jig that Rory's boy, Killian, used to do when he needed to go, and she felt the familiar stab of missing them both. "All yours," she told the mom and daughter as she stepped out of the way.

The nausea that had sent her careening out of the dining room had disappeared as soon as she'd hung her head over the toilet, with nothing—nothing!—at all happening.

It was just one more annoying thing in her life: the fact that she could be so nauseated and not actually lose her lunch. A lunch she had never gotten around to eating because she'd fallen asleep in her motel room following that meeting on the mountain. She, who hadn't indulged in naps since she'd been a three-year-old.

She reentered the dining room.

Most of the booths were now occupied and Nick had stood up and was talking to a couple sitting in one of them. When he spotted her, he waved her over. "Megan, this is J.D. and Jake Forrest. And their youngest, Tucker."

She felt aggravated by life in general at the moment, but still managed to go through the motions of being polite. "Nice to meet you." She shook their hands and exchanged smiles with the boy sitting between them. Tucker looked older than Killian by a few years, but judging by the way he was shoveling down his food, he had the same kind of insatiable appetite.

"J.D. and Jake run a horse rescue," Nick told her.

Megan's attention pricked. "Really."

"Yeah, and Nick says you're a wrangler." J.D. had

light blond hair pulled up in a ponytail and an engaging grin. "You're the one we've been hearing about who'll be working on April and Jed's place."

Megan glanced at Nick.

"Word travels in Weaver," he said wryly. "Particularly when it comes to family."

Word traveled where Megan came from, too. Which was why there wasn't a soul outside of the staff at the Wymon Women's Clinic who knew she was pregnant.

She looked again at Jake and J.D. Jake had dark hair like Nick, albeit tending toward salt-and-pepper at his temples. "Are you and Nick cousins?"

But it was J.D. who answered. "More or less. Jake's aunt Susan is married to Nick's grandfather on his dad's side. And my grandfather, Squire Clay, is married to Nick's grandmother, Gloria, on the other side."

"Unless they get divorced," Tucker muttered, not looking up from his pizza. "That's what Zach and Connor say is gonna happen."

"They're not going to get divorced," J.D. said firmly, "no matter what your big brothers seem to think. Once you see them together at the party this weekend, you'll feel better."

Tucker made a face but didn't argue.

"Squire and Gloria have been separated for a little while," Nick explained. "Anyway, our pizza's getting cold, but I thought you'd like to meet. J.D. is always looking for riders to help keep the horses exercised."

The woman nodded. "We never have enough vol-

unteers at Crossing West so you'd be more than welcome. Especially someone as experienced with horses
as you must be."

"I'll keep that in mind." It was more than a polite
response. When Megan had first agreed to return to
Weaver to work on the equestrian setup for Gage,
she'd thought she'd be facing a summer without much
opportunity to actually *be* with horses. She'd only
agreed to leave her own horse back at Angel River
because Rory's dad himself had promised to look
after her. Sean McAdams was one of the few people
Megan could always count on.

Otherwise, she'd have had to find a place to board
Earhart here in Weaver.

"Enjoy the rest of your dinner," she told them.

J.D. lifted her wineglass in salute. "You, too."

They returned to their booth and the waiting pizzas, which hadn't gotten cold at all.

Feeling suddenly ravenous, Megan stopped worrying about trying to find space for her knees without
knocking into his beneath the table. She spread her
napkin on her lap and after plucking off several basil
leaves, she eagerly took a slice. It wasn't a very big
pizza; just four pieces, meant for one person alone.
And while she'd shuddered at the notion of a meat-
covered pizza when they'd ordered, now she couldn't
help sneaking looks at Nick's.

He, on the other hand, was giving *her* a curious
look. "What was that about earlier?"

The mouthful of pizza suddenly seemed like glue.

She forced it down with a gulp of lemonade. "Just, uh, an ulcer," she lied, saying the first thing that popped into her head. "The bruschetta had some peppers that…" She trailed off because Birdie's voice was suddenly circling inside her head.

Once a liar, missy, always a liar.

Nick was eyeing her plate. She'd already eaten more than he had. "Guess you're feeling better now?"

She nodded and forced a bright smile. "Oh, yeah. Ulcer's pretty much healed. Pizza's great, by the way," she added in a rush that made her feel even more self-conscious. "A, uh, a lot better than the cup of ramen that I'd have been settling for."

"You know, there are other places you could stay besides the Cozy Night. There's a chain hotel across town now—"

"I know. But the Cozy Night's inexpensive. I don't need a lot. And the bed is comfortable enough."

She regretted the words as soon as she said them.

"I remember."

She gave him a look and he spread his hands with an innocent expression she didn't buy for a second.

She squelched a sigh and let it go, focusing on her pizza again. "Sorry about your grandparents. Being separated and all." She had no personal experience with families splitting up for the simple reason that there had been nothing to split. Her mother had abandoned Megan with Birdie when she'd been a baby. To Megan, Roberta was just a name. Which was one thing more than she knew about her nameless father. Even Birdie had never married.

Her grandmother had been an independent woman during an era when independent women weren't cool. And she'd raised Megan to be just the same.

"Gloria's actually my stepmom's grandmother," Nick said.

"Does that make it any easier?"

"Not really. It still sucks for everyone. Particularly at family events. They're both there. They're civil and all that, but everyone knows at the end of the day, she's still living somewhere other than the Double-C Ranch." He shook his head. "You'd think by the time you're their age and have been together as long as they've been together, that your relationship would be cast in stone."

"You've got a *step*mom. What about your parents?"

"My mom died when I was nineteen."

She felt a pang of guilt. "I'm sorry. I shouldn't have—"

"Don't be sorry. She was a great mom. I wouldn't be the man I am now if not for her." He sipped his beer. "Tell me about *your* family."

She picked off another piece of basil and wished she'd ordered the heart-attack special instead. "Nothing to tell." That answer seemed safe enough. "There's only me and my grandmother. She raised me. Normal family arrangements aren't really in our DNA."

"Is there such a thing as normal?"

"You know what I mean. Two parents. Two-point-five kids."

Nick just smiled and shook his head. But instead of making more of it, he pointed his fork at her plate and changed the subject. "If you don't like basil, why'd you order a cheese-and-basil pizza?"

Because at the time, it had seemed the blandest—and therefore safest—choice, considering her unpredictable morning sickness. Morning sickness that had no concept of when morning was.

"I like basil," she said. "Just don't need a whole bushel of it."

He chuckled and extended his fork. "D'you mind?" He didn't wait for a response before he scooped the fresh herbs off her plate and spread them on his slice.

"Hey! Maybe I do mind."

He raised a dark eyebrow. "Were you going to eat it?"

"No," she allowed, "but I'm not asking for something off *your* pizza."

"My pizza's hardly suitable for someone with an ulcer."

"I just *said* it was mostly healed."

"I had a roommate once with an ulcer. Guy couldn't eat anything with a hint of spice. But it's your stomach." He used his fork to scrape several chunks of sausage from his pizza onto hers. "Is that better?"

She made a grumbling sound even though it truly was *so* much better when her next bite of pizza included the slightly spicy, slightly crispy, slightly greasy sausage. Then she couldn't help but make a sound of pure enjoyment. "Should've ordered the heart attack," she mumbled when she could speak again. "Almost as good as Chef Bart's." She added the edge of crispy crust to the others that she was hoarding to save for the end.

"He's the chef at Angel River, right? Gage mentioned he was pretty impressive."

She nodded and tried not to eye the rest of Nick's pizza too noticeably. "His chocolate croissants would make you weep."

"This place doesn't have chocolate croissants, but they have pretty good cannoli."

She swallowed the last bite of her sad, sausage-free pizza and started on the crusts. "Cannoli?"

He smiled and shook his head a little before he gestured for the server and ordered dessert. Then he silently slid his plate, with the remaining slice of his pizza, toward her.

She supposed she ought to have been ladylike enough to pretend she didn't notice. But she'd never wasted a lot of time trying to be something she wasn't.

And what she *was* was still hungry.

"Thanks." She scooped up the slice and bit into its heavenliness. Her eyes might have even rolled back in her head a little.

The only thing that would have made the meal better was a frosty mug of beer. But Megan hadn't had a lick of alcohol since she'd read the results on her pregnancy-test stick.

"So," she finally said once she'd finished the rest of his pizza and all of her crusts, "what have you come up with for the barn?"

He nudged aside their empty plates and slid around the booth a few inches until he was sitting adjacent to her rather than across from her. It also meant that his thigh pressed against hers, but she was afraid if she tried to move, he'd know just how much he was disturbing her.

So she sat dead still while he grabbed one of the unused napkins and pulled his keys out of his pocket.

A stubby pen hung from the key chain.

At the sight, a smile tugged at her lips. "You're like a Boy Scout or something. Always prepared."

He gave a quick, twinkling-eyed smile, and beneath the table, Megan gouged her fingertips into her palm in a vain attempt to override the shiver suddenly rippling through her veins. Yes, the guy was still hot as ever. That didn't mean she was comfortable with her damn response.

Mercifully oblivious to her personal torment, he uncapped the pen and set aside his keys before making several quick marks on the napkin. "Construction trailer is here." He tapped one corner of the napkin. "Lodge there." He tapped the opposite corner. "Got it?"

She flattened her palm again. "It's not exactly rocket science. I think I can follow."

His lips twitched. "Okay, so the road comes up through here, where the trailer currently sits. Then it opens into parking here." He circled his pen above the white napkin. "But if we extend the road above the lodge and come back down again on the other side, to the relocated parking lot—" he made a few more lines "—then the barn that was supposed to be there can be here." He drew a quick rectangle topped by a pitched roof. "In the original location of the parking. And we can make it as big as it needs to be."

It was amazing what the man could do with a tiny Sharpie and a white napkin. In just a matter of seconds, he'd sketched out a miniature diagram of it all. "But the footprint of the parking lot is way bigger than the barn was. How—"

"Multilevel parking structure."

"Won't that be an eyesore?"

He made a face. "Come on. I graduated from Princeton. I don't design eyesores."

She, on the other hand, had graduated from Wymon High and finished her studies at that ordinary institution called life.

"And it's either this," he continued, "or make your stable multistoried. Which seems more feasible?"

"I guess the parking structure. But it seems to me that something like that is still going to detract from the beauty of the lodge itself."

"Ye of little faith." He flipped over the napkin and started fresh. He quickly drew a more detailed version of the lodge that was strongly reminiscent of the beautiful rendering in the construction trailer and then drew the parking structure, which she had to admit was almost as beautiful. He stopped only long enough to order a coffee when the server brought their cannoli and the check. "You want one?"

Regrettably, caffeine was another one of those things that she'd axed almost entirely from her diet. And she'd had a coffee—at least what could probably pass for coffee—that morning. Of course, it had come up again, but it still counted.

And it certainly hadn't done diddly to help alleviate the fatigue that seemed to plague her all the time.

"No thanks." She managed a fake smile of enthusiasm. "Another lemonade would be great, though."

"Make them to go, would you?" He handed over his credit card to the server.

"You bet," the teenager said and headed off again.

Megan told herself she ought to be relieved that their dinner together was coming to an end.

It made absolutely no sense that she wasn't.

"You don't have to pay for my meal." She flipped open her purse—basically an oversize wallet on a leather string—and pulled out some cash. "Here."

He didn't take it. And she could see by his expression that he wouldn't ever take it.

"Fine," she muttered. "Next time *I* pay."

He smiled suddenly and she realized just how easily she'd committed to a next time.

She exhaled noisily and returned her cash to her purse.

At least there was cannoli.

She bit one in half as she studied Nick's drawing again. The ricotta filling was just as creamy as it looked and studded with just the right amount of chocolate bits. "Okay, so the parking garage doesn't look like it'd be an eyesore, but it would obviously be a lot more expensive to build than just surfacing a regular old parking lot."

"Yep." He capped the pen. "But the parking needs to be accessible to the lodge. Either the traditional lot we planned all along or a vertical structure if it's moved to the other side. The whole reason the lodge is at this particular location is because it involves the least amount of blasting into the mountain. The farther up the mountain you go, the closer you get to April and Jed's cabin. Too close, and it would mean a lot more excavation. Farther down, excavation is less of an issue, but that million-dollar view is lost."

She wasn't even aware that she'd been leaning her shoulder against his until he pocketed his keys once more.

She straightened and finished the rest of her cannoli just as their server delivered the to-go cups. Nick popped his whole cannoli into his mouth and signed the credit-card slip for the meal.

She quickly grabbed the napkin with his drawings as they slid out of the booth. When they made their way out of the busy restaurant, she realized that his cousin and her family had already left, and their booth was already occupied by another family.

She felt his hand briefly on the small of her back as they went out the door, but then had to wonder if she'd imagined it as they headed for his SUV in the parking lot. She made a mental note of the brightly lit Shop-World when he drove past it. The big discount department store would come in handy for provisions for her dorm-size refrigerator back at the motel.

Milk, for instance. She was supposed to be drinking milk every day. Unless it was hot and mixed with chocolate—and ideally a generous shot of liqueur—she hated drinking milk.

She brushed aside the thought. "If you're concerned that the budget doesn't extend to a bigger barn, why consider a fancy parking garage that would cost even more?"

"My job is to figure out solutions."

"Thought your job was to not design eyesores."

"That, too."

She smiled slightly and looked out the side window. Like in many small towns, the highway ran straight through the center of Weaver and it served as the main drag. She took in the storefronts as they passed.

Feed store. Hardware store. Consignment store. The sheriff's office.

Colbys Bar & Grill.

She looked away from that one.

He stopped at one of the few stoplights in town. There was a park across the street, complete with a big gazebo outlined in tiny white lights. In the light from the old-fashioned lampposts, she saw a few joggers. A few people tossing around a ball.

She wondered how much change the town would experience because of the Rambling Mountain development.

"You know," she mused, "the barn doesn't need to have a million-dollar view."

He'd draped his wrist over the top of the steering wheel as they waited for the light to change and was tapping the dashboard with his finger. "True." He sent a smile toward her. "Told you that together we'd create something great."

She managed a smile of her own and hoped the dark would hide how weak it probably looked. If he mentioned *creating* anything together again she was going to lose her mind.

The light changed, and they soon arrived back at her motel. She was relieved.

The parking space next to her truck was now occupied by an enormous motorcycle, so he stopped behind her pickup and left his engine idling. "I'll pick you up tomorrow morning and we can head up the mountain together. I have a conference call first thing, but I should be here by ten. Does that work for you?"

She wanted to tell him no. That it did not work for her. That she'd just meet him up at the construction trailer. But there was no logical reason she could think of to argue with him.

So she just nodded and opened her door. "Thanks again for dinner."

If she'd simply left it at that, she'd have been fine.

But she looked back at him after she'd slid out of the SUV, and her mouth suddenly went dry.

The last time they'd sat in his SUV in front of her motel room, she'd confidently led the way inside.

She swallowed and moistened her lips. "Well."

He wasn't smiling now. Just watching her with those amazing gray eyes. "Well."

Her skin prickled slightly, and warmth spread through her veins again.

Invite him in. It's not as if you can get more *pregnant.*

It wasn't Birdie talking in her head this time. Just Megan's own hormones.

She swallowed again. *One and done. Remember that.* "Thanks again for dinner."

"You already said that."

She'd never been one to blush even when she'd been young and naive. If she'd ever been naive at all—not with Birdie Forrester raising her. The fact that Megan's cheeks felt warm now was as unfamiliar as everything else going on inside her.

Blasted hormones.

They were making her feel like a lunatic.

She fumbled the room key out of her pocket. It was an antiquated sort of thing. An actual key attached to an oversize diamond-shaped key ring. She held it up and rattled it. "I'll see you in the morning, then." Before she could do, say or even *think* something else, she shut the SUV door and quickly went to the sidewalk.

"Megan."

She froze when he spoke her name.

"Wear comfortable shoes tomorrow. Sturdy ones."

She had packed flip-flops and cowboy boots. In her opinion they were both comfortable. But only the boots could be considered sturdy. She nodded and continued forward.

He didn't drive away. Just remained right there, engine still running, and she cursed under her breath as she fumbled with the key twice before managing to fit it into the lock.

When she finally succeeded, she nearly fell inside the room as the door swung inward. She caught the doorknob, steadying herself, and gave a quick wave in the direction of the parking lot before shoving the door closed.

Then she stood there, not moving a muscle, until she heard his truck finally drive away.

It seemed to take forever.

Only when she could no longer hear the low rumble of the engine did she exhale. She moved to the drab brown drapes that covered the lone window and peeked out around the edge just to confirm that Nick was gone.

She let out a relieved breath and flopped onto the far bed. The one that they had *not* used back in March.

She'd been in Weaver for barely one day.

How on earth was she going to make it through the next week, much less the next few months?

Chapter Four

He was early.

The knock on her motel-room door the next morn-ing came a lot closer to nine than ten o'clock.

"Be out in a second," she yelled through the door as she pawed around in her suitcase for a fresh pair of jeans.

Of course, he'd be early.

And, of course, she'd overslept.

Her hair was still dripping down her back from her shower, for cripes' sake.

She yanked on the jeans, then caught her reflec-tion in the mirror on the wall above the plain wood dresser as she hopped around pulling them up. So far, there wasn't a single outward sign that she was preg-nant. Her jeans fit exactly the way they always had.

Her breasts didn't exceed the confines of her modest B cups yet, either.

Even when she turned to study her profile and tried pooching out her stomach, it looked as flat as ever.

When Rory had gotten pregnant with Killy, she'd had a visible bump after just eight weeks. But then again, Rory was several inches shorter than Megan's five-ten.

Her cell phone rang, nearly startling her out of her wits.

She grabbed a shirt from her suitcase, snatched up the phone from the nightstand between the two beds and looked at the number on the screen. Her grandmother.

She wrinkled her nose, debating for half a second and losing. She put the call on speaker and left the phone on the nightstand. "Morning, Birdie." She pushed her arms into her sleeves. "What's up?"

"Heard a story on the news this morning about that new Lambert State Park."

She yanked her hair out of her collar and started buttoning. "What about it?"

"Gonna be a dedication ceremony in a couple weeks. Memorial Day. Governor's s'posed to be there and everything. She's been on the news, you know. Talking about how she cares about the little towns as much as she does about the moneymakers like Jackson."

Megan frowned slightly. "Birdie, you're not interested in coming down to Weaver and attending that, are you?"

Her grandmother snorted. "Just waiting for the chips to fall. Governor seems too good to be true. You know what that means."

When Megan finished buttoning her shirt, she left the tail untucked and rooted through her suitcase for a pair of socks. "Anything that seems too good to be true usually is," she recited. "So why is it interesting enough to make you call?" Despite the fact that weeks could go by between seeing each other in person, Birdie never had much use for phone calls just for the sake of a phone call. There was always a purpose. Always a reason. Megan was like her in that way, too.

"It isn't. But I figured I'd make sure you got there okay."

She sat on the corner of her unmade bed and pulled on her socks. She eyed the phone still sitting on the nightstand. Birdie had stopped checking on Megan's whereabouts before she'd turned twenty. "Got here fine. Are you feeling okay?"

"Why wouldn't I be?" Birdie's voice was tart. "A gramma can't call and check on her only granddaughter now and then?"

Megan took Birdie off speaker and picked up the phone. She held it to her ear and went over to the window. Pulling aside the drab drapes, she looked out to see Nick sitting in his SUV. He was wearing sunglasses and wasn't looking her way.

She let the drape drop back into place and grabbed

her boots. A layer of dried mud was still caked around the edge of the soles. She tucked the phone between her ear and shoulder. "*You* don't call and check on your only granddaughter now and then."

She grabbed the ballpoint pen that sat next to the Bible inside the nightstand drawer and attacked the mud with the tip. Birdie Forrester was an independent woman. She lived alone in a small house on the same small plot of land where she'd raised Megan. But she *was* in her seventies. And Megan hadn't seen her in person in more than three weeks. "Are you *sure* everything is okay?"

"Yes. Is everything okay with *you*?"

She made a face. "Why wouldn't it be?" A thin line of mud, imprinted with the stitching from her boots, popped off and disintegrated when it hit the multicolored carpet. She grabbed the little trash can next to the dresser and discarded the mud.

"Don't be smart with me, missy. You've never left Angel River during the busy season before."

Megan picked up her second boot, this time holding it over the trash can. "Angel River's not the same anymore, either."

"Because Rory and her boy moved away."

Megan jabbed the pen into the dried mud, using it like a little pickax. "I'm coming back, Birdie. If that's what's worrying you. I'm just here for a couple months."

"I'm not worried," Birdie scoffed. "That's a waste of good energy. Well, if you see the governor at that opening, take a picture and send it to me. I'll show it off to the girls."

The "girls" were the group of women Birdie played poker with every Tuesday. And Birdie was the youngest one of the bunch.

"Will do," Megan said, but her grandmother had already hung up.

That was typical Birdie behavior.

She tossed her phone on the mattress and banged her boot a few times on the edge of the trash can. The boots were cleaner now than they usually were back in Angel River, so she called it good and shoved her feet into them. She stomped twice.

Comfortable as ever.

She put a few individually wrapped lemon drops from her rapidly dwindling supply into her pocket, grabbed her room key and her wallet from the dresser and left the room.

If she had to draw in a few steadying breaths before she reached Nick's SUV, she was the only one who needed to know.

"You're early," she said briskly when she pulled open the passenger door and slid onto the seat. She fastened her seat belt with a loud click.

"Good morning to you, too. And I called your room to let you know I was running early, but maybe you were in the shower." He waggled the phone he was holding. "Don't you have a cell phone or something?"

"Yes."

He waited, raising his eyebrows slightly.

She rattled off the number and he stored it in his phone. "But I don't usually carry it around with me," she warned.

He gave her another look. "Thereby defeating the whole purpose of having one."

She shrugged. "After losing one in Angel River during a rafting trip and another under a horse hoof, I learned it was safer—and cheaper—to leave it home." Now it was a habit. "Besides, if anyone wants to leave me a message, they do."

"Helps if you listen to phone messages," he replied. "In any case, I brought provisions." He set aside his phone and the yellow notepad filled with messy handwriting, and put a white paper bag on the console between the seats. "Help yourself."

She could smell the cinnamon even before she opened the bag. When she looked inside, she saw two pecan-studded sticky rolls. They smelled as divine as anything Chef Bart had ever whipped up. And to cap it off, the rolls were still warm. "Where'd you get these?"

"Ruby's Diner. Best breakfast in town." He tapped the coffee cup sitting in one of the SUV's cup holders. "Coffee's almost as good as the cinnamon rolls."

She put down the bag and reached for the coffee since she hadn't yet had her one cup of motel-provided instant. The cup was hot even through the corrugated cardboard sleeve imprinted with the Ruby's logo.

"There's cream and sugar in the bag with the rolls if you need it."

"Nope. Black is good." She worked open the little tab on the lid and carefully took a sip. The coffee was strong and rich and delicious, and she sighed appreciatively as it hit her system. It would be her one coffee for the day and it was a doozy, putting the instant swill from the day before to shame. "I forgive you for being early."

"I'll sleep better tonight knowing." He grabbed one of the rolls from the bag and took a large bite. Then he set it on a napkin, licked his thumb and started up the SUV. "Need to make one stop before we head up the mountain."

She thought about asking him why he hadn't made his stop before picking her up early, but she was too busy nibbling the pecans off one corner of her yeasty roll.

She needed to find her way to Ruby's Diner for sure.

Instead of turning toward the mountain when he reached the highway, he turned the other way. They passed the park again. No joggers this time. He turned down a side street, passed several churches and turned again, pulling to a stop next to a chain-link fence lined with beige material surrounding a construction zone.

He grabbed his yellow pad, wolfed down the rest of his sticky roll and pushed open his truck door. "Just gotta check a few things. Won't take long. If you want to see, you can come."

"What is it?"

"Public library."

"Your design?"

"Start to finish."

She took another bite of her roll, put it back in the bag, then got out of the SUV. With coffee cup in hand, she followed him through the opening, where a portion of fencing was pushed aside to allow trucks in and out.

There was a finished sidewalk leading to the building. Nick veered from it to speak with a husky man in overalls who was laying bricks.

More curious than she wanted to admit, she followed the sidewalk around to the side of the building that looked complete, at least from the outside. Somehow, Nick had managed to combine the modern with the rustic—the end result was all soaring windows and beautiful beams. She walked around the entire building and when she got back to the front, the bricklayer was working alone.

She went up the shallow steps that led to the library's entrance and the glass door slid open before she reached it. There were deep, comfortable chairs everywhere she looked. But the shelves didn't contain any books yet, and the study rooms weren't furnished. A wide staircase curved up one side and when she reached the second floor that looked down over the front half of the lower level, she finally spotted Nick.

He was in a far corner speaking with a gray-haired woman carrying a fat clipboard. Unlike Nick in his blue jeans and hiking boots, the woman wore a boxy blue suit that screamed she was someone official.

Megan turned away and wandered around the upper level, absently pulling her still-damp hair over her shoulder and twisting it into a braid that she had no way to fasten. The shelves up here weren't as tall as the ones on the lower level, and there were big patches of thick, colorful carpet inlaid among the wood planks of the floor. It was strikingly easy to imagine children sitting on the carpet, big picture books on their laps as they read and dreamed.

She struck the image from her mind's eye and went back down to the first floor.

Nick was crouched next to one of the windows, where he seemed to be looking at the wooden trim work. There was no sign of the gray-haired woman.

At the sound of Megan's footsteps, he straightened and smiled at her. With the morning sun shining through the window around him, he looked like he was outlined in gold.

The guy was just…beautiful.

"So?" He held out his arms. "What do you think?"

She took a quick gulp of coffee, glad he couldn't read her mind. "I like the way it's all open." She gestured toward the stairs. "Nice area up there for kids. The library in Wymon used to have just a tiny corner where all the children's books were shelved. Pretty sure I exhausted every single one that was either about horses or had a picture of horses on the cover by the time I was ten."

"My sister is horse crazy," he replied, not seeming to notice the way she was blathering. "She's driving my dad and Lucy bananas asking for one of her own."

"How old is she?"

"Thirteen. And as preoccupied with the boys in her class as with horses." He angled his head, looking toward the upper level. "Vivian was adamant about there being a large children's library. Truth is, she'd have been happy to devote the entire place to a children's library given the opportunity."

"Vivian?"

"Vivian Templeton." He began flipping to a fresh page on his pad. "She spearheaded this whole project in memory of her husband. He was a schoolteacher." Nick made a few notes, then tapped the notepad against his thigh. "Those the most comfortable things you've got, huh?" He was looking at her feet.

"Not for running a marathon, but since I don't figure on doing that, they're perfectly comfortable."

"We could stop and get you hiking boots—" He broke off at the look she gave him and shrugged. "Your feet, I guess. You ready to go up the mountain?"

"That *was* the plan," she reminded him.

"Do you ever miss a shot?"

"When it comes to humans of the male persuasion? It's as easy as aiming at fish in a barrel."

"Speaking on behalf of the male persuasion, I'm offended."

The laughter shining in his gray eyes said otherwise.

The glass door slid open smoothly as they approached it again. And it didn't make a sound as it closed after them.

"Won't it be hard to heat the place in the winter with all those windows?"

"They have more insulating factors than most of the houses around here. We're actually using something similar for the lodge up on the mountain."

"Well—" she gestured with her coffee cup "—except for the empty shelves and the landscaping outside, it looks ready to open. You've done a good job of it."

"Careful, Megan. That might be praise."

"Don't get used to it."

His smile widened. "It is just about finished. Hitting the final punch list. There's going to be a grand opening on the Fourth of July coinciding with all the other community events going on that weekend. You'll get to see Weaver at its finest." He waved at the bricklayer as they passed him again and when they reached the SUV, he pulled open the passenger door before she could reach it herself.

She usually protested that sort of thing.

Just because she had a uterus didn't mean she couldn't open her own doors. Or change her own flat tires.

Maybe pregnancy was softening her up.

She climbed into the SUV and forced herself to focus on the library building instead of Nick. "How long did it take to build?"

"Not as long as it took to design." His voice turned rueful. "Vivian had me working on it even before she got the project approved by the town." He finally pushed the door closed and she drew in a relieved breath while he rounded the front of the vehicle.

She started to reach for the white bag containing her cinnamon roll, but the smell of the cinnamon was abruptly repugnant.

She folded over the top of the bag a few times and set it behind the console in the back seat, then quickly unwrapped one of her lemon drops and popped it into her mouth just as Nick climbed behind the wheel.

He tossed aside his pad again and fastened his seat belt, then they headed off.

They retraced their route back to the highway, and he pointed out Ruby's Diner when they passed it. The restaurant was situated on a corner and would be easy for her to find on her own. From the brief glimpse she got, it looked crowded inside.

Before long, they'd left the town behind and picked up speed as the highway stretched out like a long black ribbon, cutting through the endless ranchland.

She rolled down her window a few inches, glad for the rush of air blowing over her face. Along with the tart lemon candy slowly dissolving in her mouth, it helped ease the vague churning in her stomach.

She probably should have eaten the roll *before* drinking that coffee.

He didn't seem inclined to talk and she was glad. It meant she could stare out her window and practice the whole deep-breathing thing, praying that her stomach didn't get any worse.

There wasn't a lot of traffic and they made good time. Certainly better than she had the day before when she'd driven up the unfamiliar mountain road herself.

Even though she wanted to enjoy the vista, she had to close her eyes as he drove. But then the low rumble of the engine and the rocking motion of the curves made her doze off.

She didn't even realize it, though, until she woke up and they were parked by the construction site.

"G'morning again," he said when she sat up straight. His gray eyes had that humorous twinkle and his smile was wide.

Her cheeks got hot again. At least she hadn't drooled.

Well. She was pretty sure she hadn't drooled.

She snatched her coffee cup and drained the luke-warm dregs before shoving open her door and stepping out. Only when she stood did she realize her nausea had disappeared during her catnap.

She rubbed her hands down the front of her jeans and followed him to the trailer. It felt good to stretch her legs.

Unlike the day before, the construction site was

a beehive of activity. There were dump trucks, a cement truck, excavators and backhoes. Workers wearing heavy tool belts, hard hats and safety harnesses climbed the frame of the lodge, and the sound of power tools filled the bracing air.

When she and Nick reached the construction trailer, the door was open. Several people in work clothes and hard hats occupied the desks crammed around the perimeter of the room.

Megan hung back on the plank boardwalk while Nick introduced her and then grabbed a couple water bottles from a bucket. "Come on." He brushed past her as he set off in the direction of the lodge.

With her long legs, it wasn't often that she was outpaced, yet he did it easily. She skipped a couple times in order to catch up to him. He hadn't said they'd need hard hats themselves, which meant they wouldn't be getting too close to the actual construction work. "So what's the plan now? I mean, what do we do next?"

He stopped and she very nearly bumped into him. "I want to see how much of a hike it is to get—" he pointed with one of the water bottles "—down there."

She looked where he was pointing. Beyond the lodge, the ground broke sharply downward in a mess of jagged stone, studded by trees and brush. She could see several patches of snow that still hadn't melted in the shady spots.

It was one thing to talk about moving the barn to a lower spot on the mountain. And another to actually come face-to-face with the physical challenges involved.

"You up for it?"

She grimaced. No wonder he'd warned her about her footwear. "I guess."

"It looks worse from here than it actually is."

She couldn't help a snort of laughter. She wasn't afraid of a little hike. She led them routinely at Angel River. They even had a rock-climbing wall. What they didn't have was a steep, rocky mountainside like this. "Right."

He smiled. "Trust me. I won't lead you astray." He stepped off the side of the boardwalk onto the rutted ground and extended his hand.

She took the bottle but otherwise ignored his hand, and stepped off the side, too. At least the mud had dried since the morning before. "I believe you won't walk me off a cliff," she allowed. "But trust you? Don't push it."

He pulled a face. "I'm wounded."

He so obviously wasn't. "Don't take it personally. I don't depend on others and I trust myself first. Life-long rule drilled into me by my grandmother." She twisted off the plastic bottle cap to take a quick drink. "All right, then. Lead the way."

The view as they descended was incredible, and Nick was as much a visual feast as the landscape. They slowly zigzagged down the mountain. Every time they zigged, she caught a glimpse of the distant lake beyond the trees. Every time they zagged, it disappeared from view again.

It took quite a bit of time. Not least because there wasn't an existing trail, but also because Nick kept stopping to pull out his cell phone. At first she thought he was checking for a signal, but then she realized he had some sort of app that he was checking. And he stopped to take a bit of video or snap a few photos dozens of times.

She figured they'd been at it for at least two hours before he finally came to a halt and hopped up onto a boulder that was squarely in their path. He pulled off his sunglasses and slowly turned around in a circle, nodding. "I thought this might work for the barn."

Megan didn't see how. "It's quite a hoof getting down here."

"Not so much. Come up here and see."

She was curious, so she took his hand and let him pull her up beside him. From the top of the boulder, she could see that the spot where they'd stopped was flatter than it had seemed from the ground.

He closed his hand on her shoulder and angled her slightly to the left. "We worked our way down from there. But the direct line from the lodge would be about here." He swung his arm to the right and drew a line in the air. "It's steep, but properly graded, it's wide enough for a short shuttle bus to carry people who can't or don't want to walk. This whole area's a natural shelf. Fairly level, but we never considered it for the lodge because the view isn't as good. I'll need to get the engineers up here again pretty quick, though."

She looked over her shoulder. From here, the lake appeared to be much closer, and she immediately began envisioning summer trail rides down to it. But he was right about the view. It was pretty enough but not as spectacular as the lodge's.

"We use UTVs at Angel River to move guests around," she said absently. "Could you really put a barn here? What about the riding ring?" At Angel River, they held lessons in basic horsemanship in the arena and also used it as a gathering place for dozens of activities. "Or would you want to leave the ring in the original location?"

She didn't realize that she'd been circling in place until she found herself facing Nick. She instinctively took a step away and his arm clamped around her waist when her boot found nothing but air.

His torso was hard against her chest and for a moment her mind simply went blank, surrendering to sensation.

The heat of his fingers burning through her shirt.

The rush of blood in her veins.

Then her lungs decided breathing was probably a good idea, which jarred her from her stupor.

She blinked. "Thanks." Her voice sounded softer than usual.

"Yeah." His voice sounded deeper. He cleared his throat. "We'll have to think about the riding ring."

She curled her fingers tightly, and her knuckles

pressed against his chest. The water bottle she'd forgotten she was holding crinkled loudly.

Feeling flushed, she cleared her throat, pulled away and hopped down from the boulder. She yanked off the bottle top and guzzled most of the water.

One and done. One and done.

She silently chanted the words.

Says who? Says who? her thwarted desire argued back.

Dirt and rubble scattered under Nick's hiking boots when he jumped down beside her. "You need to make a choice."

She coughed a little and swiped the back of her hand across her mouth. "About what?"

"We can take the easy route back or we can take the short route."

She swirled the inch of water still remaining in her bottle and gulped it down. "Short." The sooner they got back to the construction zone, the sooner there'd be a few dozen people around and she'd have no choice but to keep her libido in check.

Once again, Nick took the lead.

Unlike the zigzagging, almost meandering route down, the trek back up was, quite literally, *up.*

Which meant it was a lot more strenuous.

Despite the brisk temperature, there was soon a line of sweat darkening his blue T-shirt that made it cling to his long back in all sorts of interesting ways. She was sweating, too, and before long, she had to stop to roll up the sleeves of her shirt.

He paused, glancing back at her. "Okay?"

She nodded. "Just, uh, gotta catch my breath," she huffed. "You know."

"Yeah. I know." He pulled up the bottom of his T-shirt and wiped his face with it. "Warned you."

The night they'd spent together hadn't exactly been a fumble in the dark. But it hadn't been broad daylight, either. The glimpse she now got of his hard, well-defined abs was going to haunt her.

She closed her eyes and rubbed them, but the image still stuck even after she opened them again and his shirt was back where it belonged.

Why him? Why couldn't some other architect have taken over for Chance Michaels?

The universe isn't designed around your convenience, missy.

She pulled in a deep breath and blew it out hard. "Okay." She gestured at him, anxious to get moving. "I'm good. Let's go."

They set off again. At times, Nick had to pull himself up a sheer rock face and reach back down to help her.

The scrubby brush growing tenaciously on the rocky surface scraped her arms and the sharp jutting rocks scraped the rest of her.

But finally, thankfully, the ground evened out again as they reached the lodge and Megan sank down wearily on the boardwalk.

Nick went into the trailer and returned several minutes later, handing her another bottle of water.

Then he sat down beside her and stretched his legs out over the side of the boardwalk. "That was more work than I thought it'd be," he admitted.

She didn't know where the energy came from to chuckle. She drank down half the bottle before setting it aside to take off one of her boots. "I should've chosen the long route," she admitted, dropping the boot on the ground.

"Don't have blisters, do you?"

"Nah." She pulled off her other boot and rotated her ankles. "Don't think so, anyway." It was a bald-faced lie.

"Sorry."

"Not your fault."

She eased back until she was lying flat on the boardwalk staring up at the sky overhead. She saw the tops of fir trees and puffy clouds dotting the impossibly blue sky. A massive hawk glided on the breeze. Beneath the noise of hammers and guys shouting to each other, she heard the buzz of insects and the frenzied chirping of birds. "This really is a pretty spot," she murmured.

A power saw suddenly whined, drowning out the insects and the birds, and she forced herself to sit up.

She looked at her cowboy boots on the ground in front of her. At some point, she was going to have to put those things back on. The prospect held little appeal. And that was saying something, since she'd never met a pair of boots she didn't like.

She looked over at the lodge, where the power

saw was screaming. "Have they got a name for this place yet?"

He shook his head. "From what April tells me, Gage keeps making suggestions that they don't like, and she and Jed keep making suggestions that Gage doesn't like."

"Going to have to come up with something soon if they want to be able to open on schedule by fall. I'd think they'll want plenty of time to advertise and all that."

"No doubt. But that's their deal," he said. "I just need to bring the project in on budget and on time." He leaned forward, snatched up one of her boots and crouched in front of her. "Come on, Cinderella."

"I'm no more Cinderella than you are Prince Charming." But she pointed her toes and slid her foot inside the leather boot, then steeled herself as she stood and settled her heel.

"Doesn't every girl want to be Cinderella?" He held the other boot ready for her to step into it.

She snorted. "Not this girl." She eased her foot into the boot and wanted to curse when she wobbled slightly and had to steady herself with a hand on his shoulder. "Last thing I need is some man thinking I need rescuing."

He laughed softly. "Sweetheart, that is the last thing *this* man thinks where you're concerned."

The second she could, she stepped away from him and pushed her tingling fingers into her back pockets. "The last time a guy made the mistake of calling me *sweetheart*, I was sixteen." She waited a beat. "I gave him a black eye. And nobody around Wymon ever made that mistake again."

Nick had the nerve to grin. "You saying you're going to punch me in the eye—" he leaned closer "—*sweetheart*?"

She wanted to gnash her teeth. Instead she snatched up the empty water bottles and stomped off toward the trailer, annoyed as all hell because there was a weak little spot inside her that felt all gooey over that stupid, silly term.

Sweetheart.

Chapter Five

Nick gave her a ride back to the motel. The entire drive down the mountain, he peppered her with questions about how things ran at Angel River.

"I'm going back to the drawing board," he told her when he pulled into the spot next to her pickup. "Start from scratch with a new plan that'll work for the new location."

"What if the engineer tells you the new location won't work?"

"Then we'll have to take another hike."

She groaned.

"I'm kidding. No hike."

"My feet thank you," she muttered and pushed open the door. "So...what do I do now?" She'd never been involved in any sort of design process like this before. "Just sit around on my thumbs awaiting further instructions?"

"Heaven forbid you have a day to just relax," he drawled. "No. Come by my office tomorrow afternoon. I'll have initial sketches worked up by then."

"Where's your office?"

He reached into his briefcase and came up with a business card. "Anytime after three o'clock works."

She took the card, careful not to brush his fingers in the process.

Then she grabbed her wallet and stepped out of his vehicle. It was long past lunchtime and he hadn't made any mention of dinner again.

She told herself she was glad.

"See you tomorrow, then," she said briskly and shut the door. This time, she didn't fumble the room key in the lock.

"Megan, wait—"

She felt a surge of energy and looked over her shoulder to see Nick crossing toward her.

Her palm suddenly felt moist around the doorknob...

Until she saw the white paper sack that he was holding out to her.

"Your cinnamon roll," he said and pushed it into her nerveless fingers. Then he turned and loped back to his SUV, his long legs making short work of it.

Two seconds later, he was backing out of the parking spot and driving away.

That spurt of adrenaline leaked out of her, leaving her feeling even more exhausted.

She went into the motel room, which had been cleaned during her absence.

The Cozy Night was inexpensive, yes. But it still came with daily housekeeping service that, to her, was like a vacation in itself.

The trash had been emptied, the flakes of mud on the carpet vacuumed away. Her phone had been moved to the nightstand next to her bag of lemon drops.

She might miss her private cabin back at Angel River. But she definitely didn't miss having to make her own bed or vacuum up her own messes.

She dropped the white bag on the nightstand and sat down on the side of the bed to work her boots off her sore feet. She tossed the boots on the floor and carefully peeled off her socks.

As soon as she could garner enough energy, she would shower and change and then drive over to Shop-World. Replenish the lemon drops. Buy herself some blister remedies and a pair of comfortable shoes. Something between a cowboy boot and a flip-flop ought to do.

She picked up her phone and saw that she had messages. She dialed her voice mail.

"Hi, Megan." The caller had a chipper, high-pitched voice. "This is Kimmie from the Wymon Women's Clinic. Did you know that at twelve weeks, your little nugget will be the size of a plum?" The woman giggled, obviously pleased with herself. "We need to get you scheduled for your second sonogram and our first opening is at the end of the month." Her voice got even more impossibly chipper. "Don't forget to take your prenatals and give me a call as soon as you can!"

The girl was still rattling off the phone number when Megan hung up and deleted the message.

Then she tossed the phone back onto the nightstand and flopped back on the bed, throwing her arm over her eyes.

When she'd visited the women's clinic where she'd had the sonogram that only confirmed what Megan already knew—exactly how long she'd been pregnant—they'd given her a bag full of stuff. Vitamin samples. Pamphlets about this. Brochures about that.

Megan had pulled out the vitamins and shoved all the rest in a corner of her underwear drawer. When she'd packed to come to Weaver, she'd transferred the bag, along with the underwear, to her suitcase.

She had just as little enthusiasm for exploring the contents now as she had when the nurse at the clinic had pushed the bag into her numb hands.

She didn't want to think about being pregnant.

Didn't want to think about being a mother.

Undoubtedly, when Roberta Forrester had been pregnant with Megan, she'd felt the same way, because she sure hadn't wasted any time before dumping off Megan to Birdie and hitting the road.

If she'd ever told the man who'd gotten her pregnant about it, he'd never stepped forward to acknowledge it.

Megan didn't want to think there were any similarities between her and Roberta, which meant, sooner or later, she had to tell Nick.

But later.

She lifted her arm from her eyes and pressed her palms against her abdomen. "I'll get more prenatal vitamins at Shop-World, too," she whispered.

Then she turned on her side, bunched the pillow under her cheek and closed her eyes.

Nick spotted Megan's mud-spattered truck as he pulled into the lot in front of his office building. It was the only vehicle other than Gina's blue compact.

He parked in the spot marked with his name and grabbed his stuff from the back seat. His head throbbed with the headache that had plagued him all day, after spending half the night before working on the barn design and the other half dreaming about Megan.

Then this morning, he'd spent two hours trekking around on Rambling Mountain with the engineering team before he'd needed to get back to town for the council meeting.

Which meant he was short on sleep. Short on food. And short on having a solid plan worked out for Megan's barn.

Even before he pushed through the glass office door, he could see her inside, perched on one of the leather chairs in the reception area.

She was wearing dark blue jeans and a short

leather jacket over a collared white shirt. Her sunglasses were pushed onto her head, holding her long hair away from her face. And in the moment before he elbowed the door open, he saw the way she was bouncing her knee as she waited.

Her blue eyes turned toward the door as he entered to the sound of the phone ringing, and she popped out of her chair.

Agreeing to pretend there was no attraction between them was easy enough in principle. Putting it into practice was another matter when everything about her appealed to him. Not just that she was tall, leggy and a looker. Or the fact that her body and his fit so perfectly together that all his dreams for the past two and a half months had been frustrating reenactments of the night with her in room 22.

He liked her energy. Her humor and her bluntedged way with words. He didn't even mind the prickly vibe that she worked so hard to project.

It just made him want to navigate her defenses even more.

Patience.

"Hope you haven't been waiting long." He stepped inside and closed the door behind him.

"You said three o'clock," she said as if he needed any sort of reminder.

"I did." And it was straight up three o'clock right now. But he'd figured on being back to the office well before now.

Gina came around her desk and lifted the build-

ing model he was carrying out of his hands. "I told
her the council meeting was probably running long."
She set the model on the long worktable behind her
desk and snatched up the ringing phone, giving him
a harried glare. "Ventura and Ventura," she said into
the receiver.

He ignored his office manager's glare and focused
on Megan. "Do you want some coffee? Soda?"

She shook her head.

He glanced at Gina, who was listening to the caller.
"Can you hold my calls?"

She crossed her eyes at him but nodded. As he led
Megan back to his office, Gina said into the phone,
"I'm sorry, but we don't really handle custom chicken-
coop designs. If you have a computer—"

Megan made a sound and covered her mouth with
her hand. Nick saw the laughter in her eyes as he
stopped outside his open office door and gestured
for her to enter.

She went into the room and turned to him. "Chicken
coops," she said in a low voice.

"We've been asked to design doghouses," he said.
"Chicken coops are a step up." He closed the door
and swallowed a smile over how wide her eyes went.

Then she shrugged her narrow shoulders a little
and pivoted away. She seemed to be taking note of
the framed certificates hanging on the opposite wall
along with some of his favorite renderings that he'd
done over the years.

"A step up, but still beneath your big-city degrees."
She gestured at the display.

"Nothing's beneath the degrees." He deposited
his briefcase on his credenza. "But not a lot of folks
around here want to pay the going rate for doghouse
plans and the like once we've pointed out where they
can get them for free on the internet." He rolled his
stool from the drafting table to position it next to his
desk chair in front of his computer screens. "How's
your day been going so far?"

"Good enough." She didn't elaborate. But she did
perch on the stool when he patted it in invitation.
"You're looking pretty fancy. Get dressed up for the
town council meeting your secretary mentioned?"

Adding a necktie to his usual outfit of jeans and
a button-down shirt was hardly fancy. He definitely
preferred it to the suits he'd had to wear in the past.
"Don't let Gina hear you call her a secretary. She's the
office manager. And she's already pissed off because
we haven't hired someone to help with the phones."

"Keeping pretty busy even without custom coops,
I guess."

"You could say that." He sat down in the desk
chair. The stool had her sitting at a higher level
than he was and he could smell the soap she'd used.
Slightly floral. Slightly crisp.

He yanked at the knot of his tie, loosening it
enough so he could breathe again, and focused harder
on the six feet of computer screens stretched across
his desk.

He tapped a few keys to bring up the plans for the barn, starting with the basic rectangular shape. "I think I took everything you told me yesterday into consideration, but if you notice anything that seems off, just say so. Not—" he raised his hand quickly "—that I expect anything less than straight talk where you're concerned."

Her lips twitched. "Man can learn," she murmured. "Who knew?"

He suppressed a smile as he maneuvered the mouse. "So this is bare bones here. Walls. Stalls. Aisle. The aisle is wide enough to accommodate a tractor for delivering feed and hay, and hauling out waste from the stalls." She'd gone on for twenty minutes straight the day before about the importance of manure management.

J.D. was the only one he knew who talked as much or more about horse crap.

Megan leaned forward, propping her elbows on her thighs, and her hair tickled his forearm. "Twelve stalls. That's not nearly enough. That's the same number Chance Michaels originally had. I have a string of twenty-two horses at Angel River just for guests alone. And we're half the size this place is going to be."

Twenty-two. There was that damn number again. Taunting him.

"Hold on." He clicked another layer of detail into place on the screen.

"Oh." She nodded and glanced at him. The smile

in her eyes was enough to tie his gut into knots. "Twenty-four stalls. Cool."

"All based on your required dimensions, ma'am."

She propped her chin on one of her fists. "And this square here?" She circled her finger over one end of the image, not quite touching the screen. "What's that?"

"Feed and tack."

"Looks spacious enough for feed." She folded her arms over her thighs again. "Not sure about the tack, too. And depending on who they hire as barn manager, they might prefer some office space right there near the horses. I know I would."

"Surprised Gage didn't offer you that job, too."

"Barn manager?" She shook her head but didn't seem inclined to say more.

He clicked again, replacing the entire floor plan with an alternative. One central aisle lengthwise became two aisles crosswise. "We could do a second floor for office space."

"Hmm," she said softly as she studied the screen. "Yeah, maybe. I don't know."

He brought up a third idea. Totally different. Instead of stalls on either side of the aisles, they were all on one side of the aisle, which ran along the interior edge of a U-shaped building. "With this configuration, there could be even more stalls," he pointed out. "It also allows for more square footage for supplies and tack." He clicked the mouse again and another set of walls appeared. Then he adjusted the dimensions, lengthening the two opposing sides while shortening the connecting side. "If we do something like this there's still adequate room for machinery to access the stalls, and we could incorporate a third exterior door on the short side."

"Tack and feed could even be in separate areas, which I like better, anyway." She leaned forward again, and her hair brushed over his hand this time.

It was all he could do not to sift his fingers through it.

Then she pushed her hair behind her shoulder as she glanced at him. "The separate areas could be narrower. Longer. And then maybe you could add an office here." She put her hand atop his and moved the mouse pointer. Then she realized what she was doing and quickly snatched her hand away. "Sorry."

He wasn't. He finished the adjustments and she nodded, giving him a pleased look.

"I like it."

"Great." He saved the changes, then rolled his chair away from the desk, regretting the loss of contact. "I'll work on a cost estimate for this version and see where we're at."

He got up and opened his door. Across the conference area right outside, his father's office was still dark. Nick turned and leaned against the drafting table. Not once in his life had he ever been tempted to lock his door and get a woman naked inside his office, but he was now. "Engineer's report should be ready by the end of the week. If that comes back okay, we'll be set to move quickly."

"And if it doesn't come back okay?"

"Solutions," he reminded. "We'll come up with something else."

"And meanwhile? What do we do until then?"

Images filled his mind all too easily, which didn't help the way his blood had already headed south. "What do *you* want to do?"

Her lashes suddenly fell and she pushed off her stool. "Not sit around all day in my motel room *relaxing*, that's for sure. And besides, I don't think that's what Gage had in mind when he paid me for this little gig."

"I don't think he expects you to start swinging a hammer, either, sweetheart."

She gave him a baleful look. "Bet I can swing a hammer as well as you can."

He couldn't stop a laugh. He had a helluva lot of experience swinging hammers, but he didn't doubt her for a second. "I'm sure you can."

Then she shoved her hands into her back pockets and rocked on her heels, looking away. "You were right about Ruby's Diner," she said abruptly. "I had breakfast there this morning. It was really good." She waited a beat. "I actually went back for lunch."

"Oh, you're hooked now."

Her lips twitched and she pulled her hands out of her pockets. She nodded at the wall of framed renderings. "Did you draw all those?" She didn't wait for him to confirm it. "You drew the one that's in the construction trailer, too. You have a good imagination. You're quite an artist."

"Imagination is where amazing things start."

She looked thoughtful. "And that model? The one you were carrying when you came in? Did you make that, too?"

He nodded. "Vacant commercial building we're going to turn into a community athletic center."

"Isn't that what the YMCA is for?"

"If there happened to be one here. Only thing close to it is a for-profit fitness center over in Braden. Some thirty miles away. Doesn't do any good for the people living in Weaver."

"Did the town council approve it?"

"Hopefully by their next meeting they will."

"So besides the Rambling Mountain job, the library and the athletic center, what other projects are you imagining into reality?"

He crossed the office to the rear wall and pushed open the sliding door enclosing half the shelves to reveal several more models that were still in progress.

She came up next to him. "Impressive." She flipped her hair over one shoulder as she leaned closer. "What do you make them out of?"

"Depends." He snatched the knit cap of hers from the shelf before she noticed it. "These are balsa." He tapped two of the models in succession. "Medical building in Braden. Commercial complex over in Gillette." He tapped another. "Farmhouse."

"Where's that one located?"

"Outside of Weaver." He hadn't decided exactly where he'd build his place.

She straightened. "Bet you played with Erector Sets when you were little, too."

"And made model airplanes and stage sets for the drama-class productions in high school." He slid the door back in place, managing to slip the hat out of sight again. "I like using my hands."

Her gaze flickered. Then she suddenly moved away, walking over to his drafting table, effectively putting the entire length of his office between them again. She ran a fingertip along the corner of the tracing paper covering most of the surface of the slanted table. "Only things I cared about in high school were horses. Went to work for Rory's dad out at Angel River when I was fifteen. Been there ever since."

"Never got bored? Itchy for a change?"

"Nope."

"But you came here for the summer."

"For a couple months," she corrected.

"Since time is ticking away so quickly, then, when are you going to give me that dinner you owe me?"

Her gaze flew to his and her mouth opened slightly.

But whatever she'd been going to say went unsaid because Delia Templeton suddenly sailed into the room. "Hey, there, hot stuff!"

Megan's mouth closed. As did her expression.

Nick squelched his annoyance. "Delia. What're you doing here?"

And why had Gina let her back here without warning him?

"Brought you a little gift." Delia's bright eyes skipped from Nick to Megan and back again. She crossed over to him and held out a cloth-covered basket. "Montrose and Vivvie have been at each other's throats for the past day and a half." She laughed merrily. "So he's been baking off his irritation. And I know how much you love his sourdough bread."

Nick took the basket and set it next to his briefcase. "Hope you didn't make a special trip just for that, but thanks."

"Some people are worth a special trip." She walked back toward Megan and thrust out her hand. "I'm Delia, by the way. Delia Templeton."

Megan shook her hand. "Megan Forrester."

"The horse trainer. You're lucky to work with our Nick, here." Somehow, Delia managed to position herself next to him again. "He's absolutely the best." She slid her arm through his. "We're very lucky to have him."

Megan's gaze met his before flicking away. "Yes, I can see that," she said smoothly. "Well. Nick. I'll get back to you about that, uh, plan you showed me."

Before he could stop her, she disappeared through his office door.

Dammit.

His headache was back in full force. He disentangled his arm. "Delia. I was in a meeting."

"Oh, come on." She smiled, showing her dimples. "It looked like you were finished to me. And besides…" She sat on the stool and crossed one leg over the other, as if she was settling in for the duration no matter how inconvenient her timing. "My grandmother wants a report on the council meeting."

Chapter Six

It wasn't hard for Megan to find her way to J.D. Forrest's horse rescue. All she'd had to do was mention Crossing West at Ruby's Diner the next morning when she went there for breakfast, and the waitress had scrawled a quick map on a clean napkin.

Megan hadn't bothered to save *that* napkin. Unlike Nick's drawing from dinner the other night, which she'd tucked away in her suitcase for some ridiculous reason.

As she turned past the stone pillar with the words *Crossing West* engraved on it, she had to quickly revise her notion of what a horse rescue on the outskirts of Weaver might look like.

She actually lifted her foot from the gas pedal and coasted to a stop as she eyed the majestic house located on a gentle grassy rise up ahead. Three stories. Massive pillars.

The last horse rescue she'd visited north of Wymon, across the Montana border, had been stuck between a railroad track and a run-down trailer park. There had been a handful of roughly built run-in sheds and a single open pen. Despite the shoestring the place obviously ran on, it had been clean, and the poor horses well tended. But it still had been a sad, depressing place.

After the visit, she'd talked Sean McAdams into sending a shipment of feed and hay there. He'd kept up the shipments for a full year before the rescue had finally had to shut down for lack of funds.

From the looks of Crossing West, she suspected J.D. had never needed to worry about funding.

Beyond the house, she counted two riding arenas, three long barns and a verdant pasture surrounded by bright, white-railed fencing.

There were at least two dozen horses grazing.

If they were the rescues, she didn't think they looked all that poor. Not from a distance, at least.

"You're not in Kansas anymore, Toto," she murmured.

Then she pressed the gas pedal again and followed the paved road around the spectacular house until it ended in a circle near the first of the barns.

Despite the number of vehicles parked there already, she didn't see anyone around as she got out of her truck.

She could have walked straight to the barns, or even back to the house for that matter, to see if she could find an actual person, but she headed for the picturesque fencing instead.

The second she folded her arms over the top rail and propped her boot on the bottom, a gleaming bay trotted over and sniffed her arm.

They didn't have thoroughbreds at Angel River, but that didn't mean Megan didn't recognize one when she saw it. She lifted her palm and chuckled when the horse—after some initial hesitation—nudged it with his nose. "Aren't you a handsome one?"

"He's handsome, all right," J.D. called, appearing from within the barn. She was leading a small brown colt by a rope. "That's Latitude."

The second she appeared, the bay abandoned Megan and trotted along the fence line toward J.D., reaching over the top rail to bump at her shoulder.

"Be good," she chided with obvious fondness. Then she pulled a treat from her pocket and fed it to him, after which the horse pivoted on his powerful, sleek legs and ran off, his black tail streaming behind him.

J.D. was shaking her head ruefully when she reached Megan. "He's a glutton for peppermints. And I can't help spoiling him." She propped her boot on the lower rail the way that Megan had done and made a sweeping gesture with her arm. "So what do you think of our little place?" Much as Latitude had done, the young colt butted J.D. from behind until she wrapped her arm over his neck and petted him as if he was a dog.

"Little?" Megan laughed. "That's like calling Rambling Mountain a molehill. And I hope you don't mind me just showing up out here. I probably should have called first."

J.D. chuckled, waving off the concern. "Don't mind in the least. And you can blame my husband for that oversize house. When we built this place, Jake's Georgia roots were showing. His family has a long history of raising thoroughbreds. And as you can see, he just couldn't stop himself from creating a Southern horse farm like Forrest's Crossing right here in Wyoming."

Thus, Crossing West, Megan realized.

She looked around the pasture. In just that quick glimpse, she counted several thoroughbreds besides Latitude, twice as many quarter horses, a huge black Tennessee Walker and a short and stout Shetland. And—she looked twice—a llama. "Quite a variety you've got now."

J.D. nodded. "We get them from all over the United States. Abused. Abandoned. No longer wanted or whatever. We'll take them if we have room. Currently, we have eighty-seven horses. One llama. Don't ask me how many barn cats. We're pretty much at capacity until we get someone adopted out. All of these here in the front pasture are ready. Expect they'll have new homes in the next month or so. Except for Lat. He was our first and he's not going anywhere." There was obvious adoration in her eyes as she looked at the horse who was bouncing around the taller Tennessee Walker like a kid trying to coax his friend to come out to play.

"He's gorgeous." Megan wasn't exaggerating. Latitude's musculature rippled beneath his glossy reddish-brown coat. If he'd been a little leaner, he'd have looked the quintessential racehorse. "Where'd he come from?"

"Forrest's Crossing, actually. Had a brief racing career but went down when another horse collided with him. Surgery got him back up, but he was done for racing. Now he's just a pampered baby."

"I never much followed horse racing," Megan admitted. She loved horses, but more for their work and leisure aspects. "I barrel-raced when I was younger for a while."

"Me, too. Ultimately, I landed in Georgia. Worked at Forrest's Crossing as an assistant trainer for a while. That's how I met Jake. So—" she turned and looked at Megan "—what's your deal with our young Nick?"

Megan jerked slightly. "Young?"

J.D. chuckled. "Can't help it. These days that's how I see anyone who's under thirty."

Megan grimaced. Obviously, J.D. could tell that didn't apply to *her* and she suddenly felt decrepit. Just because she didn't fuss all that much with her own appearance didn't mean she had *no* vanity. "How far under thirty?"

"Just a year, but still." J.D. propped her head on

her hand. "Closer I get to the big four-oh, the more I notice youth." She wrinkled her nose playfully. "It's annoying as hell."

The other woman didn't look any older than Megan.

But then, maybe Megan should have bought night cream when she'd been buying blister bandages and prenatal vitamins.

The threat of crow's feet aside, she supposed that being three years older than Nick wasn't really so bad. At least it was better than the one time she'd hooked up with a college kid nearly ten years younger than she was. It hadn't been intentional on her part. But he'd been cute. The moment had struck and then passed, and they'd happily gone their separate ways, Megan's sexual urge satisfied for another long winter.

A portion of her mind was distracted with trying to remember what his name had been. The rest of her mind was distracted with the fact that she'd *never* be able to forget Nick.

Even if the condom hadn't failed—whichever one it had been—he was the kind of man a woman always remembered.

"There's no deal with Nick," she answered. A little belatedly, she realized, but hopefully not sounding as defensive as she felt. "Gage Stanton asked me to come and help with the design for the equestrian setup at their new guest ranch. It's what I do back at Angel River. Manage everything concerning the horses. Food. Care. Some doctoring when I need to."

She did a lot more than that, but making sure that the rotating schedule of daily guest activities stayed on track and managing the staff not directly involved with lodging and food was hardly the most interesting part of her day.

"Rambling Rad is less guest ranch and more luxury resort from what I've been hearing. Will be interesting to see how well it does around these parts."

"You don't think it'll be successful?" The thought had never occurred to Megan. In fact, there'd been a time when Gage had first come to Angel River when Rory had feared that his plans for Rambling Mountain would put them right out of business. Or that he'd intended to buy Angel River right out from under them.

"Considering the state-park thing on top of it all?" J.D. made a face. "I think it's going to be *wildly* successful. Whether or not everyone around Weaver is ready for that is another matter."

"Angel River hasn't had that huge of an effect on Wymon. Town's no bigger now than it was when I was a kid."

"Unlike Weaver, which has doubled in size since *I* was a kid." J.D. waved an encompassing arm. "Beck Ventura—Nick's dad—helped design all this."

"It looks pretty amazing," Megan said truthfully. It was like something on the cover of a magazine.

If she was going to fantasize about her dream house, though, it'd be more like that farmhouse model Nick was building. She'd have a couple horses. A dog. Maybe some chickens.

And a baby.

She rubbed the colt's back, blocking out the thought. "Is this little guy a rescue, as well?"

"Sadly." J.D. scrubbed the young horse's forehead. "A trucker found him near the Idaho border. Someone had just dumped him on the side of the highway. He was nearly starved."

"Terrible."

"He's coming along, though. Super affectionate, aren't you, buddy?" She kissed the horse on the forehead and pulled down her foot from the rail. "Come on. I'll give you the tour." She winked. "It's the price I charge for people jonesing to get on a horse."

Megan chuckled and followed. The amiable little colt trotted along. "Shows, does it?"

"Takes one to know one."

"I left Earhart at Angel River. Didn't seem fair to bring her here for just a few months. She's not a real fan of the trailer."

"Lot of horses aren't."

When they walked through the open barn door, Megan couldn't help but stop and draw in a deep breath.

Hay. Horses. If she'd have closed her eyes, she could have been standing in the horse barn at Angel River. And it coated her senses like a soothing balm.

There were only a half-dozen box stalls inside the barn. None of them were occupied, though they were all filled with fresh, fluffy straw. The rest of the space seemed to be a repository for tack.

As soothing as the distinctive barn aroma was, walking past the rows of saddles and harnesses reminded Megan yet again about yesterday afternoon in Nick's office.

And of the way the petite, curvaceous, perky Delia Templeton, of the bread and the sexy yellow sundress, had snuggled up close and comfy against him.

If Megan had needed an explanation for Nick's capitulation where her one-and-done stance was concerned, she'd certainly gotten one yesterday.

Why pursue a woman like Megan when he had one like Delia close at hand?

"You remember my son Tucker from Pizza Bella?"

Megan scrambled to get her thoughts together. The gangly boy was sitting on the ground rubbing a cloth over a finely tooled saddle. "Of course." She smiled at the kid. "Nice saddle. Yours?"

He nodded, blushing a little as he rubbed more furiously.

"Is school out already?" Megan didn't think so, but worried that her ignorance proved how unprepared she was to be responsible for another human being.

"End of next week. Kids are off today while teachers do something." J.D. grinned. "I have no idea what, quite honestly." She rumpled Tucker's hair as she passed him. "When you're finished, you can spend an hour with your precious video games."

She pushed open the door at the end of the barn when they reached it. "Given the choice, Tuck prefers video games over anything. I have a feeling he'll be more interested in going to work at Cee-Vid when he's old enough than learning how to take over the ropes here."

They passed into the sunshine again.

Thanks to Killian's last few Christmas letters to Santa, Megan knew that Cee-Vid was a video game company. She'd forgotten that it was located some-where near here.

J.D. was nodding toward the second barn they were approaching. "Keep all the equipment in here."

This time, the aroma was still familiar but not any-where near as moving. Oil. Gas. Tires. Megan glanced around at the tractors and trailers packed into the space. She had to admit that not all of the equipment looked brand-new. Or even state-of-the-art, which was sort of surprising considering the obvious money that had been sunk into the place.

The third and largest barn held only stalls. A lot of them. In fact, it was all so vast, Megan almost felt overwhelmed. She'd been to plenty of rodeos. Plenty of county fairs. But never had she seen a barn this large.

"We call this our medical wing," J.D. said, slow-ing her steps. "One of my cousins is married to a vet. He comes by at least weekly. More often, obviously, when there's a reason. Evan has a tech who is perma-nently stationed out here, though. Johnnie."

At the sound of her name, a young woman who was measuring feed from a bucket looked over with a smile.

"We'd be lost without her," J.D. added. "Johnnie, this is Megan Forrester. She's in town for a little while and thinking about volunteering some of her time here."

"Welcome, then," Johnnie said. "We couldn't operate without volunteers."

"You want to get Junior, here, settled for the afternoon? He's had a pretty good little walk around." J.D. handed over the colt's rope before leading Megan past every occupied stall, providing a brief recap of each horse's situation.

Megan's heart ached by the time they were through.

"We do everything we can to rehabilitate them," J.D. said when they finally reached the far end of the barn. "But there are some situations that can't be solved. Where neglect has gone on for so long that it can't be remedied or injuries are so severe there's no chance left for any quality of life. Then the only choice is humane euthanasia." Her expression was solemn. "Anyone who volunteers with us needs to understand that."

Megan nodded. "That's always been my stance."

J.D.'s smile returned. "Great. And fortunately, we haven't had to do that in a long while." She pushed open the final barn door, revealing another pasture; this one was divided into a series of much smaller ones. There were also several pens, most of which had a run-in shed or shelter.

And Megan saw more people here. At least a

dozen, young and old, moving among the equine patients.

"J.D., I think what you're doing is amazing." One glance told her that none of these horses were even remotely fit to be ridden. Yet. "I don't mind grooming or whatever if that's what you need me to do. God knows I know how to muck stalls, too."

She did it regularly at Angel River. As well as tossing straw and hay bales, walking miles every day and overseeing the guest activities. All for the privilege of tending their string of horses.

It'd been the perfect life.

Until her best friend and her godson had moved away.

J.D. smiled. "Someone willing to shovel horse poop. I knew there was a reason why I liked you. When do you want to start?"

Megan spread her hands and looked down at herself. She was wearing her usual Western-cut shirt and worn blue jeans. The only thing that differed from her daily attire were the tennis shoes she'd purchased at Shop-World. "I'm good to go right now if that works for you."

J.D. squeezed her arm and waved down Johnnie again. "I'll leave you with Johnnie, then. She runs the show in the med wing. When you're finished, stop off at the house. I'll introduce you to Lat's friends in the front field. They're the ones needing saddle time to keep them from getting too big for their britches."

She turned and left, and after having Megan fill

out a brief volunteer form, Johnnie continued the tour, this time stopping to go over even more details. Like which horses got which feed. Which ones needed this nutrient. Which ones needed that medication. All the details were posted neatly on a schedule, and as soon as Johnnie realized that Megan was already familiar with the task, she left her to it.

Once Megan was finished, Johnnie gave her a box of first-aid supplies and wraps, and together they tended two horses who'd been tangled in barbed wire before arriving at the rescue only a few days earlier.

After that, Megan walked several horses—some more willing than others—and cleaned hooves and brushed coats. She was patiently working burrs from an antsy pony's mane when her neck prickled and she glanced up.

Nick was standing on the other side of the pen, hands resting on the top rail. His dark hair gleamed in the slanting sunlight.

How long he'd been standing there was anyone's guess.

Heat filled her and she quickly sidestepped when the young pony jerked and kicked out a foot. The hoof glanced painfully against her leg, but she ignored it.

She'd had worse treatment.

Instead, she ran her hand soothingly over the pony's shoulder. "You're all right," she said softly.

The flesh under Megan's palm rippled and the pony yanked her head, but after a tense moment she lowered her hind leg once more.

Megan looked over at Nick again. She kept her voice pleasantly calm. Low. "What do you want?" If he said the dinner she owed him, she was going to throw the metal bucket that she'd been using to catch the burrs at his head.

She decided to blame her hostility on pregnancy hormones.

It certainly couldn't be him specifically causing it.

"Too hard to believe I don't want anything?"

She contained a snort only because she didn't want to startle the pony again.

"Does she have a name?" he asked.

"Not officially. Personally, I'm voting for Burrito."

"How'd she get all the stickers in her mane?"

"Dunno. Curiosity? I've already gotten them out of her forelock and her ears. She didn't have any in her tail." It was a tedious task, alternating between her fingers and a burr brush to separate the strands and work the prickly bits free. "Some animals have a special skill for finding the damn things. She seems to be one of them."

The entire process was a nuisance. Combine it with a skittish young pony who'd been half-starved and didn't trust anyone? Nuisance became a royal pain in the butt.

But the poor animal didn't know that.

"J.D. says you've been here nearly all day."

Better here doing something productive than sleeping the day away like a slug in her motel room. "So?"

"So don't you think it might be time to take a break?"

She lifted her head again to give him a good glare, only to realize that she was the only person left out in the pens.

All of the other volunteers had departed.

She didn't think that J.D. would have called Nick for the purpose of telling him that Megan had been there all day. "Why are you here again?"

"Checking on a delivery."

She eyed him skeptically. "Delivery of what?"

"Building trusses, actually." A smile played across his lips. "For my grandfather and Susan. They've been living with J.D. and Jake up to now, but are ready for a cottage of their own. Going to be starting construction soon." He pointed his thumb. "Right over there in the other corner of the pasture."

Now she felt supremely foolish for thinking his presence had anything to do with *her*.

She poked her finger on a lurking burr she hadn't noticed and swore under her breath when it pricked her skin. Her hands were riddled with similar jabs, but wearing the gloves she'd started out with had only made the task more difficult.

There was absolutely no reason why her eyes should sting with tears now, but they did.

She sucked the bead of blood from her knuckle and blinked, staring harder at the work still remaining. Despite the concoction of oil and hair conditioner that she'd been using along with the specially designed burr brush, she still had several inches to go and a mess of burrs and matted horsehair that was bigger than her fist.

She heard a rustle and then Nick was standing next to her. "Come on." He slipped the brush from her grip. "You can take a break."

Megan sniffled and calmed the animal again when she shifted nervously away from Nick. "If I leave her like this, her mane is only going to get tangled up all over again." Burrs were nature's Velcro. "And she doesn't like men, so don't get so close."

He obediently backed away. "Is that why she tolerates you? Because you're like-minded females?"

Megan turned away from him, swiping her nose and blinking furiously. "I don't dislike men."

"But you don't have a lot of uses for us. Except maybe one."

"Yeah, well, in my experience that's all most guys are good for." Her voice sounded thick.

"Are you crying?"

"No!" She had to quickly sidestep another kick from the pony.

He swore. "Can't you put more than one tie on her?"

"One is plenty. She's already traumatized. That's why I haven't closed the gate. Just go." She waved her arm, refusing to look at him.

God help her if she wiped her cheek.

"Leave us alone so I can finish what I started. I'm sure you've got better things to do with your time than hang around annoying me. No doubt Delia Templeton could help you with ideas." She went hot, then cold, when she heard the words come out.

And when the silence stretched out afterward, she was even more mortified.

She peered harder at Burrito's burr-ridden mane and carefully worked a lock of hair free only to feel yet another prick, this one on the inside of her wrist. She gritted her teeth and dared one more tear to slide down her cheek.

"Delia is only a friend," Nick finally said. His voice was quiet. Steady.

The kind of quiet and steady that seduced a person into believing him.

"Doesn't matter to me what she is." She knelt down long enough to grab the bottle of oily goop meant to soften the burrs and lubricate the hair. "I don't care how many girlfriends you have."

"Liar."

Despite herself, she slid a look his way, then jerked her attention back to the pony. She worked several drops of oil into the last matted knot. "If she's not your girlfriend, she obviously wants to be."

Dear god, Megan. Shut your trap!

"I've known Delia a long time. She'll lose interest before long."

Burrito jerked against her tie and lifted her back leg again. "Shhh." Megan stroked her again. "Relax. Nobody's trying to hurt you. Not here."

"I could say the same thing to you." Then he sighed

when she remained stoically silent. She heard a rustle again. "Don't stay out here all night, Megan."

She angled her head slightly, watching from the corner of her eye as he walked away.

The tear finally dared to fall.

It slid, hot and fat, right past her lashes.

Chapter Seven

Megan didn't stop at the house to say goodbye to J.D. after finally removing the last burr from the pony's mane and tucking her into her stall in the med wing.

For one thing, it was nearly dark.

For another, Megan could see through one of the windows at the back of the house that J.D. and her family—including Nick—were sitting around a big table having dinner.

She drove back into town, stopping at Shop-World yet again to pick up a small first aid kit. Between blisters on her feet and burr bites on her hands, she needed it. She also bought a quart of milk, a box of saltine crackers and a little tub of ridiculously priced facial moisturizer that was "guaranteed to reduce fine lines and wrinkles in just fourteen days!"

On the way back to the motel, she picked up a hamburger at a drive-thru. But once she drove away from the restaurant, the smell of the charbroiled beef prompted her to pull over to the side of the road and toss the burger out the window.

It was either that or pull over and toss the contents of her stomach.

At the motel, she had her pick of parking spaces. She parked directly in front of her door and carried her Shop-World purchases inside.

The room was, once again, neat as a pin.

Megan's clothes were getting more jumbled by the day inside her unpacked suitcases, however, and she promised herself that she'd hang up her stuff in the closet and put the rest away in the dresser before she went to bed.

Neat though the room was, it felt stuffy after having been closed up all day, so she propped open the door with the patio chair to get some air.

She filled the motel-supplied coffee cup with milk and drank it, then had a suspenseful several minutes before she determined it was going to stay down. After that, she rinsed out the cup and refilled it with instant lemonade.

Lemon flavor was one of the few things that seemed to unfailingly agree with her in her pregnant state.

She flipped on the television. She had no interest in watching any particular show, but it provided some welcome noise. At least enough to drown out the noise inside her head.

She grabbed the television remote and turned up the volume on Maureen O'Hara trying to slap John Wayne when he snuck a kiss.

She toed off her tennis shoes and stacked all the pillows against the cheap, fake-wood headboard. Then, with a sleeve of saltines in hand, she sat on the mattress, propped herself against the pillows and set her lemonade on the nightstand.

After sticking a cracker in her mouth, she grabbed her cell phone to check her voice mail.

"Hi, Megan," the familiar chirpy voice greeted. "Kimmie, here, from the women's clin—"

Megan deleted it.

"Hey, there, stranger. It's Rory. Gage and I are finally heading home from Maine. Give me a call. I miss you! Can't wait to hear how things are going with the Rambling Mountain deal."

Her thumb hovered over the screen to delete the message. But she didn't. She just set her phone back on her nightstand. Then she washed down the dry cracker with lemonade and leaned back against the pillows once more.

From outside, she heard the distant gunning of a car engine.

Maureen and John were still at it on the TV.

Cradling the sleeve of saltines against her belly, she closed her eyes. Just for a few minutes. Then she'd get to her suitcases...

"Holy Mother of—"

She jerked awake at the furious voice and blinked confusedly.

On the TV, John and Maureen were running into their white Irish cottage and the credits were rolling.

In the doorway of Megan's motel room, Nick was glowering.

"Anybody could have walked in here!" He kicked aside the salmon-colored chair and stepped into the room. The door shut behind him.

She swung her feet off the bed and stood up, swaying just a little from grogginess. "Anybody did!" She realized she was still clutching the sleeve of saltine crackers and tossed it onto the nightstand. "What are you *doing* here?"

"I came to check on you." His gray gaze slid over the suitcases on her bed. "Damn good thing. Snoring away. Door wide-open. Don't you have any sense at all?"

She gaped at him. "I do *not* snore."

He tossed a small plastic container onto the dresser. "Well, having witnessed more than one instance of it, I'd have to argue with you there. But the point is that you're snoozing away like the dead with the freaking door open!"

Her temper bubbled. "The *point* is that you've got no business being here at all!"

His jaw looked tight. "I brought you leftovers from J.D.'s."

"Go take care packages to your cute brunette. I don't need or want them."

"Delia Templeton is not my anything. She never has been. She never will be. I told you. She's just a friend."

"Yeah, well, if she really were *just* your friend, you'd be honest with her and tell her that, because she obviously hasn't gotten the memo!"

He pointed at her. "And if you were the least bit honest with yourself, you'd get over this stupid pretense that there's nothing between *us*."

She snatched up a tennis shoe and threw it at him.

He ducked and it hit the door behind him.

When he straightened, he no longer looked angry.

He was actually grinning.

She set her teeth, wanting in the worst way to see if her aim was any better with her second shoe. "Get. Out."

He tossed the tennis shoe back and it landed on the bed beside her. "Lock it this time." With a smirk, he went out the door and pulled it shut after him.

Megan snatched up the shoe and threw it again.

It banged loudly against the closed door and didn't provide anywhere near the satisfaction that it could have.

She stormed over and flipped the lock, then latched the door chain for good measure.

"Neanderthal!" She picked up the container of leftovers, tossed it into the empty trash can and began pacing around the room.

But the hollowness in her stomach drove her to pick the container right back out.

She sat on the foot of the bed and peeled back the lid.

A golden-brown chicken breast nestled in a bed of rice. A slice of lemon hinted at the flavor of the light sauce drizzled over it.

She put it in the microwave and set the timer for two minutes, but took it out after one because she couldn't wait.

Then she sat down on her bed and ate every bite.

After showering and slathering her face with lotion, and tending to the cuts on her hands, her bruise and her blisters, she finally, *finally*, turned off the television and the light.

She punched the pillow under her cheek.

"And I do *not* snore," she muttered.

Nick received the engineering report late the next afternoon.

He hadn't seen Megan since the night before, though he half expected her to show up at his office and give him more hell.

He was almost disappointed that she didn't.

It was much easier to deal with her ire than it was to deal with her tears.

Because whether she wanted to admit it or not, she *had* been crying out at J.D.'s over that skinny brown pony with the matted mane.

The easiest solution would be simply to call her.

Of course, she'd need to be in her motel room to actually answer either the motel phone *or* her cell phone.

"What're you looking so annoyed about?" Gina set a stack of mail on the corner of his desk.

"Seriously. What's the point of a cell phone if you never have it with you?"

She raised her eyebrows. "Okay. Well. On that note." She turned and left his office.

He rubbed his hand over his face and sighed. Then, with his briefcase and report in hand, he got up and left the office.

The phone was ringing right next to her elbow, but Gina was ignoring it, evidently in favor of popping the top of a diet soda.

"Are you going to answer that?"

She smiled. "I'm on my break. Now, if you hired someone else to help me—"

He snatched up the phone. "Ventura and Ventura." It wasn't quite a snarl.

"Nick?"

Megan's voice was immediately recognizable. And it made something tighten in his gut.

He turned his back on Gina. "Megan. Yeah. I was just heading out to—"

"I'm sorry about last night," she interrupted. Hurriedly. As if she wouldn't have been able to get the words out otherwise.

He exhaled and tapped the stapled packet of papers he was holding against his thigh.

"I didn't intend to fall asleep with the door open. And the, uh, the chicken was delicious. Anyway, I don't want to keep you. I just needed to get that out of the way."

"Okay." He shifted restlessly. "I still think you could find someplace better than the Cozy Night for the duration of your stay."

Gina wasn't making any attempt to offer him some privacy, choosing instead to make a production of unwrapping a straw and sliding it into her soda can.

He turned his back on her again. "I received the engineer's report," he told Megan. "I was actually going to head over to the motel. See if I could catch you. Are you there now?"

"How's it look?"

"Not great."

"Oh. Well. Damn."

"Yeah." He glanced at the clock. "It's nearly quitting time around here and I'm going to be busy most of the weekend." He waited a beat, then decided to just roll the dice. "How about we talk about this over dinner?" He ignored Gina's knowing smile. "You owe me one."

"After the leftovers from last night, I might owe you two. But I guess that works. Where and when?"

He wanted to say his place, but he knew she'd shy away from him as quickly as her pony had when he'd gotten too close the evening before. And he already felt as if his dice had come up doubles. "If you don't mind a drive, there's a good Chinese place over in

Braden. I have some plans I need to drop off there for a client." It was a shameless ploy—using business as a pretext—but a man had to use the tools at hand.

"The medical building?"

"Related to it. If you're able to leave soon, I'd be able to get there before his office closes."

"Well, I don't know." Her voice turned dry. "My schedule *is* pretty full."

"I'll pick you up in twenty."

"Don't be early."

He was still smiling when he turned around to drop the phone back on its cradle.

"Nicky's in luh-uv," Gina said in a singsong voice.

"It's a good thing you do an amazing job juggling everything around here for Dad and me." He grabbed one of the labeled tubes from the worktable behind her desk. "Otherwise you'd be a total pain in the butt."

The phone rang again. She smirked and lifted the receiver. "Ventura and Ventura. Well, hello, Mr. Fernandez. Yes, I have your quote all ready—"

He headed out and the door closed behind him, cutting off her voice.

He dumped everything in the back seat of his SUV and called his dad. "Sorry for the last-minute cancellation, but I can't make it tonight." His dad and a few others were meeting up at Colbys for steak and billiards.

"Everything okay?"

"Yeah. Just running David Templeton's plans over to Braden. Give him a few extra days to look 'em over before we submit them to the city." He backed out of his parking spot. "When are you going to tell Gina to place the ad for a receptionist?"

"Next week. Figured that'd be the best birthday gift we can give her."

Nick chuckled. "Speaking of gifts, what am I supposed to get Shelby?" His little sister was graduating from junior high the following week but the party was that weekend. "And don't tell me a horse."

"Got the horse covered," Beck admitted.

"She finally broke you down, huh?" He waited for a sheriff's vehicle to pass and turned out of the parking lot. "Turning into a pushover, Dad."

"Blame the women in my life. Get Shelby something for the horse," he advised. "Doesn't need to be much."

"Will do. Catch you later."

He pulled up in front of number 22 fifteen minutes later. He considered just honking to let Megan know he was here.

No doubt she would be perfectly happy—even prefer it—but it went too far against the grain for him. He figured he could learn not to open her door or pull out her chair the way he'd been taught, but there was a limit.

The drapes were pulled shut across the window of her room, so he sat in the salmon-colored chair to while away a few more minutes. Nick was pretty sure the only thing holding the chair together was all the coats of paint that had been applied over the years.

He had to give credit to the owner of the motel. At least they were trying.

The Cozy Night was located on a slight rise above Weaver and he idly watched the light traffic on the highway below. The cars were slow through town, but picked up speed as they left.

When he figured enough time had passed, he stood and knocked on the door.

Megan whipped it open immediately and stood there on the threshold. She was wearing a white collared shirt with black stitching and black jeans that emphasized her long, lean legs. Her cheeks looked flushed and her eyes shied away from his. He noticed the clothes hanging on the closet rod. Two pairs of cowboy boots and some sandals were lined up on the floor next to the dresser.

And though they were empty, the suitcases were still lying on the bed. *The* bed.

Site of unbelievable delight.

He looked from the bed to her. She was pulling her hair free of her collar and the shirt button over her breasts slipped free, allowing a brief glimpse of sheer lace beneath.

He cleared his throat slightly. "Ready?"

She nodded and started to pull the door closed behind her but darted back inside to grab the room key.

Then she yanked the door shut and stepped past him toward their vehicles. His SUV was parked next to her pickup and she hesitated in front of it, giving him a questioning look.

"At the risk of offending your sensibilities, I'll drive," he said.

"Fine with me," she said loftily. "Your SUV's more comfortable, anyway." She pulled open the passenger-side door and climbed inside.

One of these days he'd figure her out.

It was a challenge he welcomed.

He got behind the wheel and drove out of the parking lot. They were almost to the Shop-World complex before she spoke.

"How bad was the engineering report?"

"If we talk about that now, what're we going to talk about over dinner?" He reached back and blindly found the report, then handed it to her.

She flipped through the pages. "I'm sure you know all of this is basically Greek to me."

"The site we found won't work. There are a lot of reasons why in there, but the most important one is the risk of rockslides. With enough money and enough time, we could build there, but—"

"Money and time," she said, finishing for him. "So I got two blisters for nothing on that hike." She tossed the report into the back seat again. "Joy, oh, bliss."

"You said you didn't get blisters."

She just rolled her eyes.

"Anyway, it's not the end of the world. I want to revisit the idea of moving the parking lot."

He already knew the area in question was fit for extensive construction because they'd had the studies done. It would mean that the lodge couldn't be expanded farther in that direction in the future, but expanding the lodge at all was a point of some contention between Gage and Jed, anyway. Jed wanted to keep things small. Gage—being Gage—was already thinking toward the future.

"Well…"

He glanced at her when she hesitated.

"I've been thinking that maybe the barn doesn't need to be as big as I thought."

He was glad the light was red when he reached it, because it meant he could turn to stare at her. "Thinking since when?"

"Since I saw the med wing out at Crossing West."

It was his turn to roll his eyes. "No comparison, sweetheart. Even if it's doubled in size, what we're designing is nowhere as big as Crossing West."

"I know that. The place is huge. I swear I got lost twice. But it reminded me of what guests like most about the setup at Angel River. That it feels accessible. Even someone unfamiliar with horses isn't likely to feel intimidated. We want them to feel like they're somewhere special, for sure, but also somewhere they're still comfortable. Somewhere they want to visit again." The light turned green and he turned his attention back to the road. There was no such thing as rush hour in Weaver, but he knew once he got out of town, the curving stretch of highway between Weaver and Braden would be busy. "So you've changed your mind about the number of stalls or what?"

"N-o-o-o." She drew out the word as if she wasn't entirely convinced. "If the place is successful—"

"Are you beginning to doubt it?"

"Well, no. Not really." She sounded more certain again. "If they plan to utilize a similar plan as we have at Angel River, at least some of the guests will be using the horses nearly every day. There will almost always be one or two horses that can't be ridden for some reason—injuries or some other medical issue—so having the capacity to stall anywhere from thirty to fifty horses is still necessary. But maybe to keep the barn from feeling at all immense to the guests, some horses could be stabled near the lodge and some up at April and Jed's ranch. Or—" She wriggled in her seat a little, turning slightly toward him, affording him another peek of white lace. "Or maybe building closer to the lake is something we should consider. I've been learning a lot more about the state-park end of things."

"Is that what kept you occupied all day?"

"I could only spend so much time arranging my wardrobe," she said, deadpan. "Extensive as it is."

He smiled.

She rolled her window down and the breeze tugged at her hair. In March, it had been just below her shoulders. Now, only a few months later, it was quite a bit longer. She tucked it behind her ear, but it just blew loose again. "Maybe a stable near the lake could be used for more than just the paying guests. They could have rentals for people visiting the park. Or offer boarding—"

"Not much call for that around here," he interrupted. "There are already a few folks who offer boarding for those who need it. But I see where you're going with this."

He passed a slow-moving semi hauling hay and sped up slightly as the buildings, dwindling in number, fell away in his rearview mirror. "There's no road from the lodge to the lake—by design—and Jed has said flat out that there's not going to be one."

"Because?"

"He doesn't want there to be any more development than necessary, and on that side of the lake, it's his call. April's going to side with Jed on that score even if Gage disagrees. So, two to one. No road. Which leaves a several-hour hike—and a strenuous one at that—to get from the lodge to the lake, or else a good two-hour horse ride."

"So logistically, it doesn't make a lot of sense," Megan concluded.

"The only way to get to the lake is by the access road the state has put in from the highway. Whereas the road going up to the lodge and April and Jed's cabin originates a good ten miles away."

"The guy who owned that mountain didn't make things easy, did he?" she grumbled.

"Personally, I never met Otis Lambert. But from what everyone's said, he enjoyed his privacy."

"So do I, but that doesn't mean I need an entire mountain to myself to get it."

Nick chuckled. "It's easy to hear about someone who's described as a hermit. Another thing to deal with the real McCoy."

She turned back around so she was facing forward and drummed her fingers lightly on the console.

They were long. Tanned. And sported two bandages. One on her thumb. One on her ring finger.

He looked back at the road, and put his right hand on the wheel. Now his hands were in the ten-and-two position. The way his folks had taught him. But only because if he didn't keep both hands on the wheel, he was going to cover her drumming fingers with his and she'd probably tell him to turn right around and take her back to Weaver for having the gall to hold her hand.

"Do you ride?"

"If I have to." He didn't need to ask if she meant horses. There was no way she'd have meant anything but.

"*Have* to." She stopped drumming and flattened her palm against her chest. "I think my heart just died a little."

"What can I say? I rode a few times in Denver when I was a kid. You know. Birthday parties for friends or something. And that was always in an indoor riding ring. But until my dad moved here and tried his hand at being a small rancher?" He shrugged. "Not a lot of opportunity, need or interest."

"Too busy making models of skyscrapers out of Popsicle sticks, I suppose." She dropped her hand on the console again. This time, though, it was her knee that bounced.

For several miles.

It kept drawing his attention.

He turned on the radio. Thanks to satellite, his choices were a little more varied than classic country, country and new country. He settled on some Pink Floyd.

It had no effect on her bouncing knee, though.

They'd reached the halfway point to Braden when she finally stopped and folded her arms over her chest.

"I didn't go to college," she said abruptly.

He wasn't entirely sure how to respond. "Did you want to?"

"No."

She didn't *sound* defensive. "Then it worked out well."

She fell silent again for a few more miles.

"I never knew my mother." Again, her words were abrupt.

And totally out of the blue.

"I remember you mentioned that your grandmother raised you. Dad's side?"

"No. I didn't know him, either."

"Is that the reason for the lifelong lack of trust in others?"

"That and the fact that there haven't been a lot of

people around who deserved to be trusted, anyway."
She shifted. "Aside from Birdie—" She caught his
glance. "That's my grandmother. Birdie Forrester.
Aside from her, the only other people I trust with my
life are Rory and Sean. Her dad."

"Rory and Gage got married just a few months
ago, didn't they?"

"Shortly after New Year's. They had a small wedding at Angel River. They're living in Denver now.
When they're not traveling somewhere with Gage,
that is. I'm Killy's— Killian's his real name. I suppose you maybe know that."

He shook his head. "You're Killy's…?"

"Godmother."

She was back to drumming her fingertips again.
He changed the station to classical music but that
didn't have much more of an effect on her than Pink
Floyd.

"How old is he?"

"Seven."

"Do they get back to Angel River often?"

"No."

He glanced at her.

"She's planned to come a couple times, but hasn't
actually made it. Sean's gone to Denver but…" She
trailed off and shrugged.

"You haven't gone yourself?"

"Haven't had the time."

"You came here in March. Denver's less than a
day's drive from here."

She shrugged again. "I never planned to get stuck here that—" She broke off and turned her head to look out the window. Her hair blew around her head and she caught it with her hand. "I needed to get back to Angel River. Business there's been picking up again. We've been busy." She rolled up her window several inches and let go of her hair again. "How much farther to Braden?"

"Half hour or so."

"Haven't been there since I was in school. Weaver, either, for that matter. Wymon High had to travel this far lots of times to compete in sports."

"What'd you play? Basketball?"

"You assume that, why? Because I'm the giant lady?"

He gave her a look. "The only thing giant about you is your overdeveloped sense of independence. What are you? Five-nine? Five-ten?"

"Ten."

"I could still toss you over my shoulder," he said dryly. Or span her waist with his hands.

He tried to block that thought, but wasn't quick enough.

He didn't feel too bad, though. Not when he noticed that her cheeks were coloring in an interesting way.

"As it happens," she continued, "it seemed like a good idea to the basketball coach, too. But I was terrible at it. No coordination at all with the ball. Rory and I both played in the marching band."

"What'd you play?"

"Triangle."

He bit back a fresh smile. "Important role, the triangle."

"Oh, yeah." She held up her hands, miming a performance. "Band would have fallen apart without me."

"And Rory? What did she—"

"Trombone."

He couldn't help it. He laughed. He'd met Rory only once. She was probably a half foot shorter than Megan. "Between the two of you, that seems quite a picture."

She dropped her hands again, so the fingers of her left hand were resting on the console. "Yeah, well, maybe someday I'll actually show you a real picture of us from those days."

"I look forward to that."

Her cheeks colored again in that totally unexpected way and she looked away.

But her fingers weren't drumming and her knee wasn't bouncing anymore.

Chapter Eight

Nick's client turned out to be a pediatrician whose office was in a converted house.

If Megan hadn't needed to pee so badly by the time they arrived, she'd have been happy to remain in the SUV while Nick delivered his architectural plans.

Instead, she walked into the office with him and the sight of a half-dozen kids—ranging in age from infant to teenager—was enough to make her stomach want to drop out.

She had never been the sort of person prone to panic.

But all of those children, all of their energy and their runny noses and tugging on their mom's sleeves, made her suddenly want to run out of the room screaming.

Nick stood at the sliding window of the reception desk telling the receptionist the purpose of his visit, and the friendly woman gestured at the busy waiting room. "It'll be a few minutes," she said.

There were only three chairs available and none of them were next to each other. Rather than sit, Megan asked the woman in a low tone if she could use the restroom.

"Of course!" The woman pulled open the door next to her and gestured down a hallway. "Go left at the end of the hall. Then it's the last door on the right."

Not looking at Nick, Megan hurried through the doorway past the reception area and down the hall.

The restroom was painted a cheerful yellow with cartoon characters bouncing across the walls.

She peed, trying to contemplate a future full of washrooms decorated with cartoon characters and busy pediatrician's waiting rooms.

She couldn't.

She washed her hands and left the restroom.

A young mom nearly as tall as Megan was carrying a baby in a massive carrier, blocking most of the hallway. Megan hung back, trying to stay out of the way.

She glanced disinterestedly at the framed licenses hanging on the wall. They were similar to the ones hanging in Nick's office. Professional degrees. Awards.

Then she heard a bright laugh that set her teeth on edge.

Certain she had to be imagining it—that thinking about Nick's office had to be responsible—Megan looked over at the young mom again. She'd been joined by another woman.

And Megan really and truly wished that she was anywhere—*anywhere*—else.

Because that bright laugh hadn't been a figment of her imagination at all. And Delia Templeton, seemingly conjured out of nowhere, was hunched over the baby carrier.

"Oh, my god," she exclaimed. "I can't believe how much Ladd's grown since the last time I saw him!"

"Fifteen months and at the top of the growth charts," the mom said.

"Probably to be expected when my brother's the Jolly Green Giant," Delia said with that ready laugh of hers. Then she straightened from the carrier and her gaze slammed right into Megan's.

Her lips parted. She blinked slowly.

The mom glanced over her shoulder. "Oh!" She immediately stepped to one side of the hallway. "Sorry. Didn't realize I was hogging the hall here."

"No worries," Megan assured her, and started to step past them. She managed a smile at Delia that felt as awkward as it undoubtedly looked.

"What are you *doing* here?"

Megan felt like asking her the same thing. "Nick is dropping off some plans."

"*Nick's* here?"

The young mom's attention had been bouncing

back and forth between them. "I'm guessing you two know each other?"

Delia looked slightly harried. "Penny Templeton. My sister-in-law," she said. "Megan...ah—"

"Forrester," Megan said, though she felt very certain that pretty, petite Delia with the perfectly unlined face remembered her name very well. She started sidling around them, only to find her progress hampered by a tall man in a white coat who stepped out of an exam room.

"Got a logjam here," he said in a friendly tone. "Can we move things along a bit?"

"Sorry, Daddy." Delia flattened her back against the wall. "Go ahead." She shooed Megan.

Megan's lips felt tight as she tried to smile, but she finally slipped past them to return to the waiting room.

She could have cried with joy when she saw that there were no vacant chairs left, giving her an excuse to wave her hands at Nick and gesture toward the door.

"I'll wait out, uh, out—" She didn't bother finishing but headed outside before he could do more than sit forward in his chair as though he was going to stand up and offer it to her.

She skip-jogged across the crowded parking lot toward Nick's SUV, wanting to put as much distance between the building and herself as she could. This time he had locked the SUV, and she leaned her back against the passenger door, looking up at the sky.

"Why?" she said, beseeching the heavens. "Why can't there be a way to turn around in this state without running into Delia Templeton?"

The brilliant sky, with its cotton-ball clouds, provided no answer.

She exhaled loudly and ran her hand over the back of her neck, looking back at the doctor's office.

Which was clearly marked with a black-and-white sign she hadn't noticed before.

Templeton Pediatric.

She blew out another noisy breath and looked down at herself. Compared to the skinny jeans and off-one-shoulder blouse that Delia was wearing, Megan looked like a frump.

She rebuttoned the button over her nearly nonexistent cleavage and pressed her hands to her cheeks, then closed her eyes.

"Sorry that took so long."

She looked up again to see Nick striding toward her, no longer holding the long black tube containing the architectural plans. He hit his key fob and the doors of the SUV unlocked with a soft chime.

"Busy office," he said as he rounded the front of the vehicle to pull open his door. "You can see why the doc wants to expand."

She pulled open the passenger door a little belatedly and got in. "Yeah. It was…crowded." She waited for him to make some mention of Delia, but he didn't.

Penny emerged from the building before Nick finished backing out of his parking spot and the other woman offered a friendly wave as she headed to a blue van.

Nick didn't seem to notice and then it didn't matter because he was turning onto the street, leaving Penny and Delia behind. "China Palace is pretty popular. Hopefully we're early enough to get a table without too long a wait. For some reason they stopped taking reservations on Fridays."

She made a sound and wasn't really sure what she wanted it to convey. But he seemed satisfied enough.

At least he didn't give her one of those long looks that made her suspect he was trying to read her mind.

Then she wondered if Delia had hurried out to the waiting room to say hello to Nick after learning he was there.

For all Megan knew, maybe she had. Maybe she hadn't mentioned that she'd run into Megan, either.

That was very easy to believe.

And maybe Nick wasn't mentioning Delia because he—

She ground the brakes on her whirling thoughts.

Lunatic hormones.

"You didn't mention that your client was Delia's father."

"Didn't I?" He was watching the traffic, waiting to turn left at a busy intersection. "Wasn't thinking about it, I suppose." Then he glanced at her. "How'd you know Doctor T is her dad?"

She offered up a shrug as she scrambled for a plausible answer. "Heard it somewhere. I mean, that her dad's name was David Templeton. I assumed there weren't two of them."

Brilliant, Megan.

She chewed the inside of her cheek and stared out the side window at a small shopping center. It reminded her of the one in Wymon where the women's clinic was located.

She looked straight ahead out the windshield again and realized that she'd been picking at the bandage strip on her thumb so much that it was practically falling off. She peeled it away and rolled it into a rubbery ball that she squished hard between her fingers. "Do you have a lot of clients in Braden?"

"Fair number." The oncoming traffic finally broke enough to allow him to turn. "I've had jobs from pretty much all over the state."

"Do you have to travel a lot?"

"I wouldn't say a lot. But jobs need to be checked on. Most are less than a day's drive, though." He turned again, and she realized they'd already reached the restaurant.

There were dozens of vehicles parked in front of it and a small group of people congregated on the sidewalk outside the entrance.

Megan joined the queue while Nick went inside to get their name on the list. Then he returned with a menu in his hands. "In case you want to look it over."

It gave her something to do besides gnaw on whether or not he'd seen Delia at her father's office.

So she pored over the extensive menu with far more interest than she actually felt.

The group in front of them shrank before long, but another family was now behind them. Six, with four kids playfully shoving each other.

Nick's arm came around her shoulder when one of the kids ran into Megan from behind.

The frazzled-looking mom apologized, and the irritated-looking dad barked at the kids.

"It's fine," Megan told them quickly. She offered her menu to them. "Want to take a look?"

The littlest of the kids took it, and the one who seemed the oldest promptly snatched it away.

Fortunately, Nick's name was called then. His arm slid from her shoulders, but his fingers were still warm on the small of her back as she preceded him into the restaurant. They were shown to a table and Megan was glad to see that it wasn't quite as cozy as the booth at Pizza Bella had been.

"I feel a little underdressed," she said under her breath when the waiter took away the extra place settings. "Tablecloths and everything." She smoothed one hand over the linen fabric.

Nick's smile widened. "It is kind of rare around here. But you look great." The waiter returned and filled their water glasses from a tall narrow pitcher that he left sitting on the table. "You always look great," Nick added.

She wished that was true, then was irritated with herself for even thinking it.

The waiter handed them menus and Megan pretended to study hers. When he returned for their order, she was sad to have to give up the prop. Since she hadn't really been paying attention to the selections, she ordered the kung pao chicken only because she'd heard the guy one table over just order it. "Extra spicy," she added before folding her hands in her lap. She'd discarded her ruined bandage in the trash can outside the restaurant, which left her nothing to fiddle with.

"Extra spicy. Brave, considering the healing ulcer."

That's what you get for lying, missy.

She slid the linen napkin from beneath her flatware and spread it over her lap. Folded it, then unfolded it again.

Nick muttered something under his breath and leaned toward her. His large hand covered both of hers.

She froze and stared into his eyes. His face was just a few inches from hers.

"Are you always this fidgety?" he asked. "Or is it just me who brings it out in you?"

"I'm not fidgety."

His expression didn't change.

She exhaled. "Fine. It's you. Is that what you wanted to hear?"

"Why? Because of what happened in March?"

"What—what else would it be?"

His hand squeezed hers briefly before he leaned back in his chair again. "At least that's finally honest."

She swallowed, feeling miserable.

"Megan..." He hesitated, as if he was hunting for the right words to say. "I'm not going to deny that I'm interested. But if you're still worrying about me having expectations, I wish you wouldn't."

"I'm not." Her voice sounded brittle even to her own ears. "Let's just—just talk about the barn. That's supposed to be the topic of the hour."

"Yeah." He pushed his fingers through his hair. "The barn."

So they did.

He even went back out to his SUV to get that yellow notepad of his and flipped to a fresh page to make more notes.

Considering how precise his architectural drawings were and how beautiful his artistic renderings were, his handwriting was almost appalling.

And though it took a while, Megan was able to forget her uptightness. Forget just how enormous the secret was that she wasn't willing to share yet.

But by the time they'd worked their way through her kung pao—spicy enough to make her eyes water—and his tofu-and-vegetable stir-fry, they'd moved on from the pro-and-con debate over where the structure should be located.

And agreed on a spot very near where it had been planned all along.

"Well, I guess you can give me hell now since we've essentially wasted the last week," she conceded. "Since I was the one who insisted the barn needed to be bigger in the first place."

"Solutions, remember? Good or bad, every idea we've tossed around this past week has landed us here." He tapped the rough sketch he'd made of the new plan. "With something neither one of us had in our minds from the outset. And—" he smiled at her "—if we go with more prefab elements like you were just talking about, our timeline might even be shorter."

The waiter appeared by their tableside. "Can I get you anything else? Another dessert? Refills?"

Megan realized then just how long she and Nick had been commandeering their table. Outside the restaurant windows, it was dark. But the long line of people waiting for a table was easily visible through them. "No thank you." She reached for the black folder that he'd left sitting near Nick several glasses of lemonade ago. "Nick?"

"Agreed," he said, and she had the distinct feeling that he was struggling not to pick up the dinner tab.

But he didn't.

She paid the bill, leaving an extragenerous tip because of the amount of time they'd hogged the table.

Once they were headed back to Weaver, she couldn't help a yawn before they'd even been on the road for ten minutes.

"Sleepy?"

"Full." She patted her stomach, then blinked her way through another yawn.

Nick chuckled. "Give it another hour. Food'll wear off." He turned down the radio until it was little more than a gloss over the muted sound of the engine and the tires on the road.

"I can't believe I didn't suggest a shed row before now." She shook her head.

"Neither did anyone else," he pointed out. "We were collectively stuck on the aisle-barn idea. It won't take me much time to work up the new design. The structure will be long as hell, but with just the single row of stalls—"

"Enclosed," she reminded him. Which was a bit of a turn on the traditional shed row.

"Enclosed," he agreed. "And we can run the turn-out alongside the road."

"And everyone who drives up to the lodge can admire the horses along the way. First they'll see the riding arena. Then another curve in the road and they'll see the stables."

She could picture it very clearly in her mind. Even the horses would be afforded the million-dollar view, whether they were in their stalls or out in the spacious grassy turnout area right next to them.

"We can stake it out first thing Monday morning."

"Sounds good." She rested her head against the seatback and watched the taillights of the vehicle ahead of them. "And I'll get in touch with the guy I know at Duncan Custom about the stall gates and the rest of the accessories. This would be a big job for them, but they've always been able to deliver in a

very short time when I've worked with them before."
She stifled another yawn—badly—behind the back
of her hand. "Sorry."

"You're going to have me yawning, too, in a minute," he warned easily. "Might get dicey on this particular road."

The road was narrow, steep in spots and riddled
with curves. "I trust your driving."

"Well, hey. Mark the calendar. She actually trusts
me."

She smiled. "Truthfully, though, the highway here's
almost as bad as the road going up to the lodge."

"Which was a helluva lot worse before you even
saw it in March. By then we'd added several more
safety rails and widened a few passes where they
could be widened."

"I don't think I'd have wanted to see the road any
earlier than I did," Megan admitted. She yawned a
third time. "Good grief," she muttered.

The sound of his deep, soft chuckle curled around
her senses.

"The road out to Angel River isn't nearly as difficult. It's just long and boring until you hit the river
valley. And then it's—" She shook her head and
sighed slightly, envisioning the river and the trees
and the cabins spread out like jewels on a bracelet.
"It's like you've landed in a little corner of heaven."

"Already missing it, are you?"

She'd expected to. But half of what she missed

most about Angel River was now in Denver. "I've only just gotten here this week," she replied.

The taillights were beginning to mesmerize her, and she blinked hard, pushing herself upright a little more because she'd been slouching forward. "We don't have to wait until Monday to stake it out. It's not like I'm doing anything else this weekend." Then she remembered and waved her hand. "Forget that. You already said you were busy this weekend."

"Shelby's graduating from junior high next Friday. She's having her party this Sunday. I need to get a gift first."

"This is your horse-crazy sister you're talking about?"

He chuckled again. That deep, sexy, nerve-soothing, gut-tightening chuckle. "One and the same. I have another sister, too. Sunny, but she came along after my dad married Lucy."

"Do you know what you're going to get Shelby?"

"Nope. My dad admitted they're surprising her with a horse, though."

"Lucky girl. I didn't have my own horse until I'd been living at Angel River for five years. Earhart."

"As in Amelia?"

She nodded. "I still have her. Just get your sister something for the horse. Saddle. Blanket. There are endless possibilities there."

"That's what my dad suggested, too. Problem is, I have to actually *choose* one of those possibilities and there's not a lot of time between now and then."

She felt his glance. "You were a thirteen-year-old girl once. What did you like then? And please don't tell me thirteen-year-old boys."

She laughed outright. "I'm afraid that may leave me with nothing else to suggest."

He groaned.

She pointed a finger at him. "You were no different and don't pretend you were. In fact, you were probably worse. Only thing boys that age are thinking of is sex. In double fact—" she jabbed her fingertip into his arm "—the only thing boys of all ages are thinking about is sex. I mean, generally speaking." She wanted to smack herself in the head for even getting on to the topic.

Generalizations or not.

The truck in front of them suddenly turned off the highway and she gripped her armrests tightly as she peered out at the spot where the taillights had disappeared. "I hope there was a road there."

"There is. Quite a few of them, in fact. There are turnoffs all the way to Weaver. A couple cattle ranches. At least one sheep farm that I know of. Lot of pretty land, actually. And convenient living midway between Weaver and Braden. What one town doesn't have, the other one does."

She relaxed. "Like Chinese food." She watched him in the light from the dashboard. "You *do* live in Weaver, don't you? I mean, you're not driving me all the way to the Cozy Night just to have to turn around again and drive—"

"I live in Weaver." He'd cut her off, sounding amused. "I have a condo not all that far from Shop-World."

"A *condo*." She shuddered. "Seriously? You're an architect!"

"Architects can't live in condos?" There was mocking laughter in his tone.

"Well, obviously, they can live wherever they want." She angled herself in the seat and tucked her hand beneath her cheek. "Just seems an unexpected choice in your case."

Again with the chuckle that sent slippery warmth through her. "It's temporary. Until I find the right place to build my personal dream."

"What're you looking for?"

He didn't answer immediately. He glanced her way. "I'll know it when I see it."

She swallowed and faced forward again.

But the damage was done. His words seemed to echo in the space between them all the rest of the way to Weaver.

She was never so glad to see the neon Cozy Night sign in her life.

Nor had she ever been so grateful when he didn't pull into the empty parking spot next to her truck after he drove into the lot.

If he had, it would have been way too easy for him to turn off the engine.

To come into the room with her...

She unsnapped her seat belt. No amount of will-power would block the erotic images inside her head. "Thanks for dinner."

"Isn't that supposed to be my line tonight?"

"Okay, thanks for driving us to dinner." She shoved open the passenger door and got out. "I'll see you up on the mountain first thing Monday morning." She started to close the door.

"Megan."

Every cell she possessed went still. She was hovering on a precipice that felt as seductive as it was dangerous.

"Come with me to Shelby's party."

She tightened her fingers around the strap of her purse. "I don't think that's a good idea, Nick."

"It's just a bunch of family and some friends."

Friends like Delia?

"April and Jed will be there," he added. "They'll be interested to hear what we're thinking on the barn. And I can introduce you to Axel Clay. He's a breeder you're going to want to meet. Does a lot of horse trading, too."

She felt as deflated as a million balloons popped by sharp pins.

Business.

Of course.

It's what she wanted, wasn't it? To keep things on a business footing?

"Just say yes, Megan," he said quietly. "It's not that hard. And I can guarantee the good food. There's always *lots* of good food."

She pressed her lips together.

But even though she shook her head, the word that finally came out was *yes*.

Chapter Nine

Even though she'd agreed to go to the party for Nick's sister, Megan insisted on getting herself there.

And so, on Sunday, she arrived alone at the massive home belonging to Nick's folks where a hoard of people had congregated beneath the brilliant blue sky.

It's just a bunch of family and some friends, Nick had said.

More like half the town.

She'd had to park quite a distance down the gravel road, behind a long row of vehicles that had arrived before her. As a result, she'd also had ten extra minutes while she walked the rest of the way to the house to silently berate herself for agreeing so easily to come.

Simply because Nick asked.

She hadn't even seen him yet; it was April who spotted her and introduced her to the soon-to-be, junior-high graduate. "Megan's in town for a couple months doing some work with us up on the mountain," she told Shelby, and the girl nodded, the hint of confusion in her eyes clearing.

"I wondered if he'd gotten a new girlfriend and didn't tell me!" Shelby Ventura's brown hair was lighter than Nick's and her eyes were golden brown. Her shorts were short and her top was cropped.

Unlike Megan, who had felt self-conscious about her similarly angular figure at the same age, Shelby just showed hers off with enviable naturalness.

"Not a girlfriend." Megan managed a laugh and hoped she didn't look as awkward as she felt. She extended the small box wrapped in bright blue paper and topped with a curling mop of white ribbons. "Congratulations."

Shelby possessed her brother's ready smile. "You didn't have to bring a gift."

"I heard this is your junior-high graduation party." Megan pointedly looked at the gift-laden table behind the girl. "To me that means gifts are definitely required."

Shelby laughed. "It looks too pretty to open."

"I'd take credit for that, but honestly, it was the girl at Classic Charms who deserves it." Thanks to the advice of the waitress in Ruby's Diner, Megan had visited the eclectic shop in search of an appropriate gift for a teenage girl she'd never met. She hoped that

Loyal Readers
FREE BOOKS Voucher

We're giving away THOUSANDS of FREE BOOKS

Romance

Wholesome Romance

Don't Miss Out! Send for Your Free Books Today!

Get up to 4
FREE FABULOUS BOOKS
You Love!

To thank you for being a loyal reader we'd like to send you up to 4 FREE BOOKS, absolutely free.

Just write "YES" on the Loyal Reader Voucher and we'll send you up to 4 Free Books and Free Mystery Gifts, altogether worth over $20, as a way of saying thank you for being a loyal reader.

Try **Harlequin® Special Edition** books featuring comfort and strength in the support of loved ones and enjoying the journey no matter what life throws your way.

Try **Harlequin® Heartwarming™ Larger-Print** books featuring uplifting stories where the bonds of friendship, family and community unite.

Or **TRY BOTH!**

We are so glad you love the books as much as we do and can't wait to send you great new books.

So don't miss out, return your Loyal Reader Voucher Today!

Pam Powers

LOYAL READER
FREE BOOKS VOUCHER

▼ DETACH AND MAIL CARD TODAY! ▼

YES! I Love Reading, please send me up to 4 FREE BOOKS and Free Mystery Gifts from the series I select.

Just write in "YES" on the dotted line below then return this card today and we'll send your free books & gifts asap!

→ YES ←

Which do you prefer?

☐ **Harlequin®
Special Edition**
235/335 HDL GRGZ

☐ **Harlequin
Heartwarming®
Larger-Print**
161/361 HDL GRGZ

☐ **BOTH**
235/335 & 161/361
HDL GRHD

FIRST NAME	LAST NAME

ADDRESS

APT.#	CITY

STATE/PROV.	ZIP/POSTAL CODE

EMAIL ☐ Please check this box if you would like to receive newsletters and promotional emails from Harlequin Enterprises ULC and its affiliates. You can unsubscribe anytime.

Your Privacy – Your information is being collected by Harlequin Enterprises ULC, operating as Harlequin Reader Service. For a complete summary of the information we collect, how we use this information and to whom it is disclosed, please visit our privacy notice located at https://corporate.harlequin.com/privacy-notice. From time to time we may also exchange your personal information with reputable third parties. If you wish to opt out of this sharing of your personal information, please visit www.readerservice.com/consumerschoice or call 1-800-873-8635. **Notice to California Residents** – Under California law, you have specific rights to control and access your data. For more information on these rights and how to exercise them, visit https://corporate.harlequin.com/california-privacy.

© 2021 HARLEQUIN ENTERPRISES ULC
® and ™ are trademarks owned by Harlequin Enterprises ULC. Printed in the U.S.A.

SE/HW-820-LR21

HARLEQUIN® Reader Service —**Here's how it works:**

Accepting your 2 free books and 2 free gifts (gifts valued at approximately $10.00 retail) places you under no obligation to buy anything. You may keep the books and gifts and return the shipping statement marked "cancel." If you do not cancel, approximately one month later we'll send you more books from the series you have chosen, and bill you at our low, subscribers-only discount price. Harlequin® Special Edition books consist of 6 books per month and cost $4.99 each in the U.S or $5.74 each in Canada, a savings of at least 17% off the cover price. Harlequin® Heartwarming™ Large-Print books consist of 4 books per month and cost just $5.74 in the U.S. or $6.24 each in Canada, a savings of at least 21% off the cover price. It's quite a bargain! Shipping and handling is just 50¢ per book in the U.S. and $1.25 per book in Canada*. You may return any shipment at our expense and cancel at any time — or you may continue to receive monthly shipments at our low, subscribers-only discount price plus shipping and handling. *Terms and prices subject to change without notice. Prices do not include sales taxes which will be charged (if applicable) based on your state or country of residence. Canadian residents will be charged applicable taxes. Offer not valid in Quebec. Books received may not be as shown. All orders subject to approval. Credit or debit balances in a customer's account(s) may be offset by any other outstanding balance owed by or to the customer. Please allow 3 to 4 weeks for delivery. Offer available while quantities last. **Your Privacy** – Your information is being collected by Harlequin Enterprises ULC, operating as Harlequin Reader Service. For a complete summary of the information we collect, how we use this information and to whom it is disclosed, please visit our privacy notice located at https://corporate.harlequin.com/privacy-notice. From time to time we may also exchange your personal information with reputable third parties. If you wish to opt out of this sharing of your personal information, please visit www.readerservice.com/consumerschoice or call 1-800-873-8635. **Notice to California Residents** – Under California law, you have specific rights to control and access your data. For more information on these rights and how to exercise them, visit https://corporate.harlequin.com/california-privacy.

▲ If offer card is missing write to: Harlequin Reader Service, P.O. Box 1341, Buffalo, NY 14240-8531 or visit www.ReaderService.com ▲

BUSINESS REPLY MAIL
FIRST-CLASS MAIL   PERMIT NO. 717   BUFFALO, NY

POSTAGE WILL BE PAID BY ADDRESSEE

HARLEQUIN READER SERVICE
PO BOX 1341
BUFFALO NY 14240-8571

NO POSTAGE
NECESSARY
IF MAILED
IN THE
UNITED STATES

Shelby liked the glass horse figurine she'd found as much as she did.

She started when she felt a hand on her shoulder and swallowed a protest when Nick put his arm around her.

"I see you've met already." In honor of the exceptionally pleasant afternoon, he was wearing cargo shorts and a T-shirt that clung in every distracting way that a T-shirt possibly could.

More distracting than that, though, was the cute little girl clinging to his back like a limpet. She looked like a miniature female version of him, from the deep brown hair to the dove-gray eyes.

"Sorry I didn't catch you when you arrived," he said. He bounced the girl on his back and she squealed excitedly. "Sunny, here, was keeping me busy."

If their baby is a girl, will she look as much like Nick as Sunny?

The thought was disturbing. Mostly because of how dangerously sweet it felt.

As did his companionable arm on her shoulders.

"I'm a big girl." Megan took a step sideways—and out from beneath that arm—to place her gift among the jumble of others on the table. Closer to the house, several other tables were covered with pink cloths and trays of food. Huge bouquets of pink and purple helium balloons were anchored from the table corners.

Music was playing loudly and at least a dozen kids—as varied in ages as those in the doctor's office—were chasing each other around with water pistols, screeching and laughing.

"Chloe's looking for you," Nick told Shelby almost as if that had been his reason for appearing in the first place. "She was with Dillon."

The girl's eyes widened and she immediately pivoted on the heel of her sparkle-studded sandal. But then she skidded to a stop and looked at Megan again. "Thank you for coming," she said in a polite rush before she darted away.

"Shelby likes Dillon," Sunny said importantly. "But *I'm* gonna marry him."

Nick's eyebrows rose as he looked over his shoulder at the girl. "You're six years old, kiddo. What're you doing talking about marrying anyone?"

"He shares his cookies with me." She patted his cheek as if the answer was obvious. "Nicky, I want down."

He swung her off his back and she smoothed her frilly red-and-white polka-dotted dress before dashing off after her big sister.

Nick looked at Megan. "I don't know whether to laugh or lock her up."

"She's definitely a cutie. Both of your sisters are." *Those are your baby's aunts, missy.*

She pushed her hands into her back pockets and avoided his eyes. "Nice place your folks have."

"Yeah. Dad built it from the ground up, but Lucy's added her touch since they got married." He glanced around. "Come on. I'll introduce you."

"Oh, but—"

It was too late. He'd already grabbed her elbow and was towing her toward the food tables. An older version of Nick manned a charcoal grill while an ethereal-looking blonde next to him waited with a big platter in her hands.

"Dad. Luce." Nick's grip wasn't hard, but it wasn't going anywhere, either. "This is Megan Forrester."

The blonde smiled widely. "The horse trainer!" She set aside her platter and stuck out a graceful, narrow hand. "We're so pleased to meet you. Nicky's talked of nothing but you for weeks now."

Nicky looked chagrined. "Megan. This is Lucy. My beautiful but bigmouthed stepmother. And my dad. Beck Ventura."

Megan shook Lucy's hand, then Beck's. "Pleased to meet you." She looked around her. "You have a lovely place here," she added. "And your daughters are both sweet."

"Sunny announced that she intends to marry Dillon McCray," Nick said. "Just wanted to warn you."

Lucy picked up her platter again. "Last week she wanted to marry Eli Scalise." Her laughing eyes met Megan's. "But since he's already twenty—and therefore old—she decided she needed to focus on someone younger."

Beck, however, was shaking his head and groaning. "Our daughters are making *me* old." He gestured with his barbecue tongs. "You like steak, Megan? First batch is almost ready."

Ordinarily, Megan loved steak. But the fragrant smoke rising from the grill was doing a number on her stomach.

"We'll get it on the second round," Nick said before she could figure out a polite way to decline. "I want to introduce Megan around first."

Without waiting for them to comment, he drew Megan away again. "I saw Axel driving up not too long ago. He's the breeder I was telling you about. Works with his dad."

"Clay Farms," Megan said with a nod. "I'd heard of them even before I got involved with Gage's deal. But Sean's always had me deal with a trader out of Montana whenever we've needed to acquire a horse for Angel River."

"Were you wanting to use the same place for here?"

"That's kind of up to Gage and those two." She nodded toward April and Jed, who were sitting at a picnic table with a handful of other people. "They're the ones writing the check."

"Axel's a cousin," Nick said, as if that would settle it.

"Around this place, the term *cousin* seems to cover a *lot* of ground."

"Oh, yeah," he agreed humorously. "But it's easier than saying someone is your half cousin by marriage once removed or something equally confusing." He waved his arm, encompassing the crowd. "I like to think of the family tree more like a family garden.

Lots of stuff that belongs there whether it's sprouted naturally or was transplanted."

Megan's stomach fluttered nervously. Her family garden would have one more now. Birdie. Megan.

Baby.

She realized she'd pressed her hand to her stomach and quickly shifted her fingers to her hip. She could see Shelby and a few other girls about her age preening for a clique of boys who seemed oblivious. "Is the you-know-what still a surprise?"

He nodded. "Lucy's parents are supposed to deliver the package sometime this afternoon. Cage and Belle have been hiding the you-know-what at their ranch for the last few days."

"What did *you* end up getting her?"

"A horse blanket. It's a god-awful shade of pink with some sparkly kind of stitching."

If the girl's glittery sandals and the plethora of pink and purple party decorations were any indication, Nick's choice would be right up Shelby's alley.

"Yo, Nick!" Two tall, handsome teenagers who were obviously twins jogged past, tossing a football between them. "You up for a rematch?"

"You'll still lose," Nick told them, without breaking stride.

Their derisive hoots floated in their wake.

"That was Zach and Connor," Nick told her.

"J.D.'s boys?"

"None other."

"Good-looking kids." She watched them toss the ball back to another teenager about the same age.

"They're hellions," Nick said wryly. He didn't seem to notice that his hand had found hers.

Megan certainly had.

But try as she might to make herself pull her hand away, she felt as giddy as Shelby had looked when she'd run off to find Dillon.

What followed then was a veritable parade of faces and names that Megan didn't have a hope of retaining.

On one side of the grassy lawn, she met April's grandmother, Gloria, whose hair had probably been as brilliantly auburn in her day as April's. On the other side of the party, she met Squire, the intimidatingly fierce gray-haired man who was Gloria's estranged husband.

And in all the green acreage between them, Megan met aunts of so-and-so. Uncles of someone else. And, of course, cousins.

Lots and lots of cousins.

She talked equine traits with Axel, tractors with Jed and the merits of checkers versus chess with Nick's grandfather Stan.

But when Nick nudged a plate containing a thick slab of oozing grilled meat into her hand, she had to beg off.

"Sorry." She realized she couldn't even look at the steak without feeling her stomach rise up in her throat. "Where's the—?"

"Right inside the back door," April told her, obviously recognizing the urgency. And Megan bolted.

She thought she heard Nick say something about "ulcer" before she raced into the house.

Fortunately, the powder room really was just inside the back door of the house.

And it was unoccupied.

Unfortunately, the small, open window high up on the wall allowed that ordinarily delicious aroma of grilling steak to flow right into the small room.

It did *not* help the situation.

After she threw up, all she wanted to do was curl up weakly on the cool tiles of the pretty room. But she knew that if she didn't get herself together, Nick would come looking.

She dragged herself up to the sink. Her face looked pale in the mirror, but otherwise pretty normal. Too long a nose. Too wide a mouth. Ordinary blue eyes. And tiny lines her new night cream hadn't yet eradicated.

She smoothed the front of the red blouse she'd trotted out in honor of the party and raked her fingers through her hair until it was lying smooth, more or less, behind her shoulders.

A stack of violently pink paper guest towels sat on the marble vanity top and she used more than her fair share to wash and dry her face. She rinsed her mouth as best she could, and with her very last lemon drop tucked inside her cheek, she went back out to brave the world.

She nearly bumped into Gloria and Squire, who were squaring off in the kitchen.

They'd obviously been arguing but went silent at the sight of Megan.

"'Scuse me," Megan murmured hastily and escaped out through the back door.

The lid on the grill was shut; Nick's father was no longer tending it. It was quickly obvious why—Shelby was over at the table of gifts, opening them.

Megan knew if she tried making her escape from the party altogether while everyone was conveniently occupied, Nick would make a big deal of it later on.

Birdie always said to hold your head high no matter what the gossips were saying.

Megan wasn't vain enough to figure anyone was gossiping about her, but she straightened her shoulders, anyway, as she crossed the green grass toward the crowd surrounding Shelby and her gifts.

Nick immediately materialized at her side even though she'd chosen to hang back behind everyone else. "You okay?"

She pushed the lemon drop from one cheek to the other with her tongue and nodded.

"Maybe you should see someone," he suggested. "Obviously that ulcer isn't as healed as you say. Lucy's brother's a doct—"

"I'm *fine*."

He looked ready to argue, but Shelby suddenly screeched because she'd noticed the horse that her grandfather was leading into view.

Megan loved horses. Any breed. Any color.

But even she knew there was something magical about a palomino. Particularly to a thirteen-year-old girl.

The elegant Morgan horse possessed a golden yellow coat and flowing white mane and tail. She looked absolutely perfect in every way and there was a collective "awww" when Shelby burst into tears and leaped right up into her grandpa's arms.

Megan looked down at the toes of her boots—she'd even polished them for the occasion—and quickly swiped a finger under her lashes.

"Are you crying again?"

She whipped up her head and almost choked on her melting lemon drop. "I never cry."

Nick leaned closer to her ear. "You never snore, either." Then he gave a soft *oomph* when her elbow hit him in the stomach.

Smirking, she walked away, aiming for the food tables, where she glanced over the offerings. Steak was out of the question, of course, and the deviled eggs arranged on a tray nestled in ice were a close second.

But there was a bowl of fresh melon and berries that looked appealing and Megan dropped a big spoonful onto her paper plate. She chose a lemon-lime drink from a barrel of melting ice containing canned soda and bottles of flavored water, then carried everything to one of the picnic tables that had been abandoned during the excitement over the gifts.

Her shoulders stiffened when she heard a rustle

behind her, but it was Gloria Clay. She was holding
one of the flavored waters and she smiled as she sat
down across from Megan and situated her floaty floral dress around her.

"Those melons are a good choice." The gentle lines
arrowing out from Gloria's eyes deepened slightly
with her smile. "Doesn't change too much when it's
coming up."

Megan grimaced at this proof that the woman had
heard her retching in the powder room, and Gloria
reached over to pat her arm. "Don't be embarrassed,
sweetie. I was a nurse for a long time." Her gaze
drifted, following Squire as he approached the white-
maned horse.

Megan automatically glanced that way, too. The
tall lean man carried a cane but didn't particularly
look as if he needed to use it.

She focused again on her fruit salad and opened
the can of icy soda.

"I also raised two daughters." Gloria's attention
had snapped back to Megan. She waited a beat. "Who
are raising their own now, as well," she added.

There was nothing at all similar between Gloria
Clay and Birdie Forrester. Not their looks. Definitely
not their manner. There was no earthly way that this
woman she'd just met could know that Megan was
pregnant, any more than Birdie could know.

But even though *ulcer* was screaming inside Megan's head, something about Gloria prevented her
from actually uttering the lie.

She also didn't seem able to utter anything else because her mind was an absolute blank.

So she offered what she hoped passed for a smile and shoved another chunk of melon into her mouth. And was impossibly grateful when Nick tossed a paper plate on the table next to hers and sat down.

She didn't even necessarily mind the sight of the chargrilled steak that covered half of it. Or the fact that his warm shoulder bumped against hers.

Close by, Shelby was now astride the horse's bare back while Squire held the lead.

"I drove by the library the other day," Gloria said brightly. She swept a lock of hair away from her cheek and tucked it into the clip holding the rest of the wavy mass at the back of her head. "It all looks magnificent, Nick. Vivian must be very pleased."

Megan would have had to be blind to miss the wary look Nick shot toward Squire.

But his voice was natural enough when he answered. "Very pleased."

"Is there anything I can do for the grand opening? I'd be happy to volunteer in some way."

Megan could have sworn the woman raised her voice so that it would carry. Meanwhile, Nick shifted and his thigh pressed against hers.

"I'll pass that along to Delia. She's supposed to be in charge of those particular moving parts."

"Good to know. I know you see her often. Be sure and give her my best." Gloria stood and her dress swished around her legs. Her smile was wide. Bright.

"The things Vivian has done for this town are nothing short of remarkable."

She turned then, her dress practically floating, and seemed to almost skip over to Shelby and the horse. "I want to get a picture of the two of us, sweetheart. Squire—" she held out a cell phone "—you don't mind, do you?"

Nick made a sound under his breath and attacked his steak. Megan couldn't help being impressed that the steak seemed to cut like butter despite the plastic knife and fork he was using.

Even though she knew it wasn't any of her business—at all—she leaned against him, keeping her voice low. "What's going on there?"

"Stupidity," he answered back, keeping his voice equally low. "And pride."

Megan noted that Squire had taken the cell phone, though he made no pretense of being happy about it. She heard "infernal device" more than once, as well as a few colorful curses while he captured a photo of his preening wife and great-granddaughter.

Then he shoved the phone back into Gloria's hand and stomped off.

Megan watched him go. "Does he ever actually *use* the cane for walking? Or just to make sure nobody gets in his way?" The man didn't literally whack anyone with the long piece of knotty wood, but he definitely waved it a few times to clear a path for himself.

"No." Somehow, Nick's hand had landed lightly on her thigh, and she felt the imprint of each warm finger right through the denim. "And yeah. Pretty much." With his fork, he stabbed a chunk of watermelon from her plate and ate it.

"I beg your pardon?"

His eyes were alight. "Good watermelon."

"Yes. *My* watermelon." She pointed her own fork in the direction of the food. "There's plenty of it right over there if you want your own."

"But it wouldn't be as good as yours."

She rolled her eyes. "Eat your own food."

"Whatever you say." He grinned and shoved another bite of the tender-looking beef into his mouth.

But his hand didn't leave her thigh.

And she didn't fuss or protest at all.

Chapter Ten

"Catch that tie over there on that corner stake," Nick yelled from where he stood nearly half a football field away.

It was eleven in the morning. A thick layer of gray cloud shrouded much of Rambling Mountain, a far cry from the brilliant blue sky that blessed Shelby's party the day before. The wind was so strong that it snatched the barricade tape right out of their hands every time they tried to get it attached to the stakes that they'd spent the last hour pounding into the ground.

Megan danced around, trying to catch the lightweight orange ribbon whipping above her head. She finally succeeded and, hunching her back against the wind, tied it yet again around the corner post and hastily tacked it in with several construction staples. She straightened and waved the stapler, indicating success. "Got it!"

On the other end, Nick was playing his own game of chase-the-tape. She huddled in her jacket, moving from side to side as she stomped her feet, trying to stay warm.

She'd been born and raised in Wyoming. She knew the vagaries of weather very well.

But they *never* had wind like this in Wymon or Angel River.

She squinted through the hair blowing across her face, watching the crew working on the lodge. The cold temperature and gusting wind weren't standing in their way at all.

Since last week, the bare bones of the frame had gradually been covered up by the exterior sheathing. Now it was easy to see where the doors were going to be. How immense the windows would be.

In contrast, the lean rectangular outline that she and Nick were constructing was nothing but a series of wooden stakes and bright orange tape.

For the last two hours, he'd measured. Then pounded in a stake. Then measured again. He'd moved stakes. Measured more. Taken more notes. Yes, the entire thing was on an incline from its highest point near the construction trailer to its farthest point some distance down the road. But based on the beautiful new drawing Nick had posted in the trailer that morning, Megan could tell that the design was going to work perfectly.

In reality, it wouldn't just be a single barn. It would be a series of them, with several spacious stalls each, arranged neatly down the incline. He'd done the same design for the storage buildings that would house the office, all the tack and equipment and everything else needed for the care and feeding of the horses.

And the overall structures echoed the spectacular beauty of the lodge itself.

She hadn't even wanted to look at the architectural plans.

Hadn't needed to.

Because what he'd drawn on paper had even exceeded the images she'd formed in her mind.

She was sorry that she wouldn't still be there to see it once it was completed and occupied by its new equine residents. But when that day arrived, her job would be finished and it would be up to the new barn manager to enjoy. She would be back in Angel River.

Alone.

She pushed away the thought.

He jogged back up to where she was still stomping around to prevent her feet from becoming blocks of ice and tossed the few wood stakes they hadn't used off to one side.

Unlike her, he'd been smart enough to wear a knit cap pulled down over his brow. His cheeks were ruddy, and the gray of his eyes was lighter than the cloudy sky. "What d'you think?"

She tucked her chin into the upturned collar of her jacket. "Looks perfect."

Nobody needed to know that she wasn't just talking about the staked-out barns.

"I think so, too." He stuffed his notepad under his arm and started walking back uphill. They both had to lean into the wind to make any progress and when they reached the construction trailer and he held open the door for her, she dashed inside.

And was immediately surrounded by warmth.

She dropped the heavy stapler into the toolbox and rolled one of the desk chairs closer to the wall unit providing all of that welcome heat. "So now what do we do next?"

"Huddle together to stay warm?"

Something inside her fluttered and it had nothing to do with morning sickness.

She glanced at the heating unit behind her. "Got that covered already."

Flashing a smile, he tossed the barricade tape and his pad on the desk nearest the door. Then he pulled off his cap and stuffed it into the pocket of his vest. His dark, messy hair tumbled over his forehead.

"Next—" he turned up one flannel sleeve a few turns "—there's more paperwork to be filed. More government tape to deal with."

She'd leaned over to grab the tape when it rolled off the desk. "Hope it won't be as bad as what we just went through out there with this stuff." She set the thick spool on the desk next to her.

He rolled up his other sleeve and poured himself a cup of coffee. Still holding the glass carafe, he gave her a questioning look.

She shook her head. "Already had my allotment for the day."

"Just as well." He took a sip. "It's not like Ruby's." He spun one of the chairs around and sat down, propping a sturdy work boot on his knee. "Once we get an official okay to proceed—"

"How long do you think that'll take?"

"Could be a week. Could be a month."

"A month!" She pushed out of her chair. "I might as well go back to Angel River if I'm going to be sitting on my thumbs for that long."

"It's unlikely that it will take that long, but it's still a possibility. A lot depends on how well I do my job." He flicked the thick sheaf of plans spread across the desk. "Fortunately, we're not starting from scratch like we were with the entire development plan. And, meanwhile, there's plenty to keep you busy when it comes to the barn interior. Choices for materials. Stall accessories. The whole prefab thing when it comes to stall enclosures and gates or whether a hybrid approach is better. We're going to want to meet with the builder on that."

The door to the trailer opened, and they both looked over as April Dalloway hurried inside.

"*Freezing* out there," she said breathlessly. She closed the door and unwound the brilliant blue scarf from around her head and neck. "June is only a little ways away, so naturally the weather has to take a nosedive." She flipped her hair behind her shoulders and unzipped her coat. "Thought I'd come down and take a look at the progress. The lodge is really taking shape! I hope it doesn't rain again and slow things down."

Given how dark the clouds were, Megan wasn't optimistic on that score. But she didn't want anything impeding their progress, either.

"I took some pictures of what you staked out there." April waved her cell phone. "I've already sent them to Jed and Gage." She leaned back against the desk near Nick and crossed her ankles. "Have fun at the party yesterday?"

She was looking at Megan.

"Yeah. It was…it was nice."

"Gorgeous horse for Shelby," April said to Nick. "Come from Axel's place?"

"Where else?"

April's gaze bounced back to Megan. "Let me know when you want to go out there. I'd like to go with you."

"Of course. I hadn't made any firm plan yet, but—"

April lifted her cell phone and grinned. "Easily taken care of." She started tapping on the screen. "No reason for you to monopolize every minute of Megan's time, is there, Nick?"

"I suppose I could share her for a while." His gaze slid over Megan, making her feel even warmer than the heater did.

April held the phone to her ear. "Hey. You have some pretty ponies I can come look at? This afternoon? Tomorrow?" She listened for a moment, then nodded. "That works. See you then." She slid the phone back into her coat pocket. "This afternoon," she said, straightening from the desk. "We'll have lunch first," she added and gave Nick a sideways look. "Girls' lunch, so don't think you're going to butt in the way you tend to do."

"Isn't that sexist these days?"

She wrinkled her nose at him. "Whether it is or not, you and your dad are meeting up with Jed at the Rad this afternoon, anyway. So why go down the mountain, only to have to turn around and come back up?" She looked at the round utilitarian clock hanging on the wall. "If we leave now, we'll still get to Ruby's before it closes." She looked at Megan and began winding her scarf around her neck again. "Have you been to Ruby's yet?"

Megan nodded. Just the thought of the Reuben sandwich there was enough to make her mouth water. She stood up. "I have my own truck up here, so I'll have to follow you down."

April dropped a kiss on Nick's cheek and pulled open the trailer door, which allowed a gust of wind to blast through, scattering papers left and right. "Yikes." She ducked her head and hurried out.

"Drive carefully," he warned Megan as she followed.

"I'm always careful."

Then why are you two and a half months pregnant, missy?

She yanked the door closed after her and shielded her eyes from the wind as she hurried along the boardwalk after April toward their vehicles.

The wind buffeted her truck as she followed April's sporty red SUV down the winding road, but it began to die down the more they descended toward the highway. By the time Megan pulled into a slanted parking spot against the curb half a block from the diner, at least her knuckles were no longer white.

They had to wait a few minutes for a table, so Megan went to use the restroom. When she came back, April was sitting at one of the corner booths.

Tina, the same waitress who'd recommended the Classic Charms shop to Megan, took their order and hurried away.

"So," April said as she doctored her iced tea. "How're things going with Nick?"

The words were straightforward enough. But the I-know-what-you-did-last-March singsong quality, along with April's sly smile added an entirely different spin.

"They're fine," Megan said as if she didn't have a clue what April meant.

"Oh, come on." April wasn't going to give up quite that easily. "You know what I mean."

"And there's nothing to say," Megan insisted. For some reason she thought of Rory and all the times she'd egged on her friend when it came to the subject of her budding romance with Gage.

"He's a great guy, you know. Honest. Brave. The real true blue."

Sexy as all hell.

Megan smoothed the paper napkin over her lap. "You sound like his campaign manager and he's running for local office. Which means there's some scandal in there that you're hiding."

April laughed. "I've known Nick for ten years. Trust me. No scandal. No secrets. The guy is as upfront as it's possible to get."

No secrets.

That didn't make Megan feel too great.

At least she managed not to run her finger beneath the suddenly too-tight collar of her thin turtleneck. "What happened to Chance Michaels, anyway?"

"Ah. Good old Chance." April rolled her eyes and shook her head. "His wife found out he was cheating on her and took off with everything they owned. He headed off down to Florida to convince her it was all some big mistake."

"Was it?"

"Not if Janine Crowley's obviously pregnant belly is anything to go by. She's a cocktail waitress at JoJo's. Chance was a regular patron there." She looked disgusted. "The dimwit. Chance, I mean. Not Janine."

Megan tugged on her turtleneck.

April probably didn't notice because just then the

waitress returned with their food. She barely paused as she slid the sandwich baskets onto their table.

Megan immediately tucked in. It was the first full meal she'd had since her bout at the party and she felt ravenous. April must have felt the same, because she focused on her food, too, much to Megan's relief.

When they were finished with the meal, Megan climbed into April's SUV and they drove out to Clay Farms, where they found Axel Clay watching over a newborn foal.

April and Megan both hung over the side of the foaling stall to watch the little brown girl work so hard to get up on her spindly legs. With her back legs finally braced wide, her front legs looked as if they'd give out. Then she plopped down in the straw only to try to stand yet again. And again. Until finally, she was on all fours, big eyes swiveling around for her mama, who'd alternated between cleaning her newborn and backing away to give her the space and encouragement she needed to find her first meal.

"I want her," April said when the foal was finally nursing. She was smiling through her tears.

"You want every foal you've ever laid eyes on," Axel responded. "And you can't have her, 'cause she's already promised to a client."

"*I'm* a client," April reminded him.

"I do have a few others," he said dryly and shook Megan's hand. "Let's go back to the office and talk about what you're looking for up at the—" He glanced at April. "What *are* you going to call the place?"

April wrinkled her nose. "Very good question. I told Gage the other day we're going to end up pulling a random name from a hat at this rate."

"Rambling Mountain Resort doesn't do it for you?" Axel looked like he wanted to laugh. "Just go with the obvious, I say."

"Like Clay Horse Farms?"

"It says who and what we are, doesn't it?" He led the way to a tidy office half the size of the foaling stall where Megan happily spent the rest of the afternoon looking through the records of all the horses already entered in the sale they'd be having in August.

Megan didn't plan to still be there by the time of the sale, but that didn't preclude her from choosing from the offerings beforehand, and she felt like they'd come up with a solid place to start by the time April dropped her off at her truck, still parked outside of the now-closed Ruby's Diner. It would necessitate a few trips out of town to see some of the animals Axel thought she would like, but that was fine with Megan.

Maybe with a little breathing space, she would be able to get her senses back under control where Nick was concerned. Maybe she'd be able to figure out how she was going to tell him about the baby without causing him to cut and run the way her father and her grandfather had done.

It was raining by the time she let herself into her motel room. She shrugged out of her jacket and kicked off her boots before turning the knob on the unit beneath the window from cool to heat. She hoped it would actually produce some warmth after all the shuddering and groaning, because the room was barely any warmer than outside.

Despite the Reuben at Ruby's earlier that day, her stomach was growling in a way that no instant ramen cup would satisfy, so she ordered a pizza before dealing with her voice mail.

She listened to Kimmie's latest message, which was really more of a lecture delivered in her high-pitched chipmunk tone regarding the importance of proper prenatal care.

Megan returned the call but only reached the voice mail because the women's clinic had already closed for the day. She left a message for Kimmie that she was seeing a doctor elsewhere and hung up.

And then, because her conscience nagged her, she yanked out the inch-thick phone book from the nightstand drawer, found a listing for a doctor in Braden who did *not* share the Templeton name and left a message to make an appointment. There was no way she'd see a doctor in Weaver.

With her luck the doctor would turn out to be yet another one of Nick's "cousins."

The window unit was still huffing and wheezing but producing no measurable heat yet, so she took a hot shower that steamed up not only the minuscule bathroom, but also a good portion of the room.

She wrapped her hair in a towel and pulled on a pair of sweatpants and a thermal long-sleeved undershirt. Then she propped herself up on the pillows and got under the blanket she dragged from the extra bed before picking up her phone again.

Feeling annoyingly nervous, she dialed Rory's number.

What would she say to her friend?

You found a husband when you weren't looking. But I did you one better—I'm pregnant.

She swallowed hard when the ringing stopped, and Rory answered. "Hello!"

Megan steeled herself. *Just blurt it out.* "Hey, you're never—"

"Sorry that I've missed your call, but you know the drill. Leave a message!"

The beep sounded.

"Hey," Megan repeated, trying to force some cheer into her tone. "Just…just calling you back. Finally." She cleared her throat. There was no way she could tell Rory she was pregnant in a voice mail. "Tell the gorgeous Gage that his equestrian facilities here are going to be amazing. Like the angels from Angel River took flight up here or something." She thumped herself on the forehead. Attempts at poetic imagery were as unlikely from her as pointless phone calls. "Anyway…" Her throat felt a little tight. "Give Killy a kiss for me and, um…" She cleared her throat. "I miss you guys, too."

She hung up and thumped her head against the pillow behind her, then nearly jumped out of her skin when she heard a knock on her door.

"Pizza Bella," the muffled voice called through the door.

Oh, the pizza. Duh. She shoved aside the blanket to grab some cash from her wallet for the driver's tip before yanking open the door.

Only it was Nick who was standing there.

Nick, wearing a tan all-weather coat with the collar flipped up over a dark sweater and black jeans, looking like an ad from some highfalutin outdoor-gear place. Water streamed down from the edge of his umbrella. He was holding the pizza box.

Megan looked past him. "Where's the delivery guy?"

"On his way to his next delivery." He pushed the box into her hand. "You gonna let a guy in out of the rain or what?"

She stepped back, feeling unsettled.

He entered, collapsing the umbrella and leaving it propped against the door after he closed it. "How'd it go out at Axel's?"

"Fine." She ran her fingers along the edge of the cardboard box. "What're you doing here? And don't say you've picked up a new side hustle because you need the delivery tips." She was glad she'd paid for the pizza over the phone when she'd ordered it, at least. Otherwise, she'd be beholden to Nick for another meal.

Despite the umbrella, his hair glimmered with drops of rain, which made the dark strands look even richer. "I wanted to drop these off." He pulled several catalogs from inside his jacket, where he'd obviously been protecting them from the rain. "Cabinetry." He tossed them on the extra bed. "If you want to take a look and see if anything strikes your fancy."

She lifted an eyebrow and the towel wrapped around her hair began slipping down her forehead. "For the horse barn?"

"What else? You wanted an office. And the feed needs to be stored in something."

She slid the pizza box onto the dresser and read-justed the towel on her head. She felt as if he'd caught her wearing only a towel. As it stood, he was dressed in a coat that probably cost an arm and a leg and she was wearing faded sweats that she'd owned for ten years. "I had something more utilitarian in mind than *cabinetry*."

"Steel shelves and five-gallon buckets, I suppose."

"Something wrong with that?"

"Form follows function. Doesn't mean it shouldn't look good in the proc—" He broke off and pulled his cell phone out of his pocket. "Sorry." He frowned slightly. "I'd better—" He didn't finish, but just held the phone to his ear. "Hey, Delia. What's up?"

Megan leaned against the dresser, deciding abruptly that if he wanted privacy for his call, he could go right back out into the rain.

He looked up at the ceiling, then around at the window unit, which sounded like it was suffocating. "Tell Vivian everything's on track and I'll call her back when I have a chance. Yeah. I'll see you later."

He pocketed the phone again. "Sorry about that. It's cold in here."

"How can you tell?" She gestured at his coat.

His gaze slid over her. "I can tell."

Beneath the ancient, soft waffle-weave shirt, her nipples tightened even more. She crossed her arms, but he'd turned away to poke at the buttons of the heating unit.

"That's not gonna help," she told him. "Already tried."

"Have you told the office?"

"I'm not complaining about that thing. They'd probably want me to move to a different room and—in case you haven't noticed—it's raining."

"Admit it." He shot her a wicked grin. "You'd miss our memories from room number twenty-two."

The thought was alarming.

What if he was right?

"Get over yourself." She carried the pizza box over to her pillow-mounded bed and arranged herself once more with the extra blanket. Then she flipped open the box and removed a slice of the heart-attack special.

The first bite was as divine as she'd anticipated. "Oh, *yes*," she said around her mouthful.

He swore at the asthmatic window unit and straightened.

"Told you." She considered offering him a piece of the pizza but decided that it was probably safer all around if she didn't. "So what're you all dressed up for," she asked. "Hot date with Delia?"

"Yeah, right. I'm heading to Gillette." He raked back his hair, and the glimmering specks of rainwater disappeared.

She was itching to run her fingers through his hair, too, but shoved another bite of pizza in her mouth instead.

A woman needed to satisfy at least *some* of her cravings.

"That's one of the reasons I wanted to drop off the catalogs. I'll be gone for a few days."

"What were the other reasons?"

His eyebrows came down. "What?"

"Never mind."

He paced around the bed—*the* bed—as if he didn't want to get too close to it.

She knew the feeling. So why *hadn't* she requested another room by now? The only days the Cozy Night didn't have any vacancies were weekends.

"You could stay at my place. At least it's got a freaking thermostat that works."

Her legs came down off the bed and the pizza box slid alarmingly close to the edge of the mattress. She rescued it and placed it safely on the middle of the bed. "No thanks."

"I'm not even going to be there!"

"And when you're back? What then?"

He sighed noisily and yanked his cuff, glancing at the sturdy watch on his wrist. "I need to get going."

"Late for that date?"

"Keep bringing that up and I'll start thinking you're jealous."

She gave him a look and took an enormous bite of pizza. Better to keep her mouth too full to talk.

Only problem with that was not choking when he stepped between the beds and leaned over her, arms braced on the mattress next to her hip.

Then, she didn't dare move.

Chew. Breathe.

"You *could* pretend that you'll miss me a little bit." His voice was low. Deep.

He leaned even closer.

Her heart slammed against her ribs, and heat rushed through her veins. It pulsed in her breasts and pooled between her thighs.

He lifted his hand.

She was weak. If he so much as touched her, she was going to pull him down with her, and then she'd have two damn beds in this room where she didn't have a hope in Hades of getting a peaceful night's rest.

His hand passed through the air two inches above her aching breasts.

He reached into the pizza box and pulled out a slice.

Then he straightened and she couldn't help wondering whether she was imagining the devil in his eyes or not.

He toasted her with the slice and devoured it in

a few bites, right up to the crispy edge of the delectable crust.

A crust that—he leaned over her again—he tossed back in the box.

Definitely with the devil in his eyes.

Which set off a fresh conflagration inside her.

By some grace, he turned away, and missed the hand she'd stretched out toward him.

Her fingers curled and she shoved her hand down next to her thigh.

Bad fingers.

He tucked his umbrella under his arm. "Try to stay out of trouble until I get back."

She gave a derisive sniff. "Right."

His teeth flashed, then he pulled open the door and a fresh stream of wet air rushed into the room before he left.

With the door closed once more, her room felt cold all over again. Cold and empty.

Trouble?

Megan sank back against her pillows and shivered. She flattened her hand against her heart.

That horse has already escaped the barn.

Chapter Eleven

"All right." Dr. Natalie Ambrose snapped off her gloves as she pulled down the paper that was draped over Megan's legs and rolled away on her low stool. "Everything's looking great, Megan." She disposed of her gloves and washed her hands in a small sink. "Any questions?"

Other than how did I get myself into this?

Megan shook her head. She was still feeling choked up from hearing the baby's heartbeat.

It had sounded like galloping hooves.

Everything else the doctor had done during the exam had been entirely mundane in comparison.

"You can get dressed and I'll meet you in my office when you're ready."

Megan waited for the doctor to leave the examining room before she pushed herself up from the table. She yanked off the paper robe and pitched it in the trash, then put on her jeans and sweatshirt.

It had been three weeks since she'd left the message to get an appointment with the ob-gyn. Three weeks since Nick had shown up at her motel room to let her know he'd be gone for a "few" days.

Oh, he'd called her a *few* times from Gillette, where he'd said one of his jobs had hit a serious snag.

Once to let her know that the building plans for the stables were officially a "go."

Once to ask if she'd enjoyed the town's Memorial Day celebration and meeting the governor at the state-park dedication. April and Jed must have told him about that.

After those first two calls, Megan had faced up to the horrifying fact that she missed him.

Not just the way she'd missed seeing Rory and Killy after they'd moved to Denver with Gage.

The way Megan missed Nick was keener. With a far sharper edge that wasn't familiar—or welcome— at all.

And before Nick's third call—just two days ago— Megan had learned that someone else was also out of town.

Delia Templeton.

Megan learned that thanks to the chatter at Ruby's Diner, where she'd fallen into the habit of lunching after her daily visit to the construction site.

"She off with Vivian?" Bubba, the tatted-up cook,

had poked his head like a turtle out the kitchen's pass-through to ask the question.

The waitress who'd delivered the news had shaken her head. "I don't think so."

"Off chasing after Nick Ventura again, I'll bet. That's a girl on the hunt," said the woman sitting next to Megan at the counter. Dori worked at the bank down the street.

"Like Howard Grimes has been on the hunt after you?" Bubba had guffawed and pulled his head back into his shell while Dori blushed.

Three weeks of nearly nonstop noontime lunches at Ruby's had not only made Megan's jeans fit more snugly, but they'd also taught her that gossip in Ruby's was a pastime treasured by the locals as much as, or more than, the food.

Telling herself that she didn't give a flying fig whom Nick spent his time with was fine and dandy as long as she didn't give herself a moment to acknowledge what a big fat lie it was.

So when Nick had called for the third time that very same evening, Megan turned off her cell phone unanswered and shoved it into the nightstand drawer.

She had to admit that her mood had been pretty bad ever since.

This was why she knew better than to get emotional where a man was concerned. She was a Forrester. And Forrester women didn't do relationships.

When she reached Dr. Ambrose's office, the middle-aged woman wasn't there.

Megan sat in one of the two chairs facing the desk and crossed her legs. Uncrossed them. Recrossed them.

She pushed to her feet and restlessly prowled out to the hallway. She could hear the murmur of voices but no sign of the doctor.

She returned to perch on the chair again. The doctor had a large anatomy model of a pregnant torso sitting on the corner of her desk. Megan touched the model baby curled inside the uterus and it tumbled out. She tried to catch it, but it squirted out of her hand onto the carpet just as Dr. Ambrose walked into the office.

Megan smiled weakly when the doctor picked up the plastic baby. "Sorry."

"Happens all the time," Dr. Ambrose assured her. She popped the model baby back where it belonged. "Fortunately, the real thing doesn't usually tumble out of place so readily." She sat behind her desk and adjusted her eyeglasses as she studied the medical file she opened. "Before you leave today, my nurse will get you set up for your next prenatal check in four weeks. She'll also get you scheduled for your sonogram, which will be—" she glanced at a little chart "—the last week of July." She closed the manila folder and smiled. "Even if your partner can't join you for your regular checks, I really encourage him to attend the ultrasound appointment. It's an exciting moment seeing your baby for the first time. Have you been giving some thought to whether you want to know the baby's sex?"

Megan shifted uncomfortably. "I actually live up near Wymon," she said. "I'm not sure if I'll still be down here by then or not."

The doctor nodded, not seeming surprised. "Schedule the sonogram, anyway," she advised. "It's a lot easier to cancel the appointment than it would be to fit one in on short notice when there's no emergency." She made a note on the file. "Do you have any questions? Concerns?"

Megan's gaze snuck to the baby in the model. "Shouldn't I start showing soon? My waistband is barely getting tight."

Dr. Ambrose's smile widened. "I know some moms who would envy you. You're taller than average, Megan. And frankly, a little underweight. We'll watch that, of course, but right now there's no reason to worry about your baby's development. Your pregnancy is exactly where it should be. And one morning soon, you'll wake up and you suddenly won't be able to zip your jeans. Just have patience."

Naturally, the doctor thought Megan was anxious to begin looking the part of pregnant mom.

"Here's a prescription for your prenatal vitamins. The over-the-counter brand you've been taking is adequate, but these are still my recommendation." Dr. Ambrose passed Megan a slip of paper. "Occasional dizziness. Mood swings. Headaches. Appetite fluctuations. Decreased sex drive. Increased sex drive. All of these things are very normal right now."

Megan folded the square piece of paper and slipped it into her wallet. What she'd like to have would be *no* sex drive. Maybe then she'd stop dreaming about Nick's hands on her.

And stop caring whether or not he was off with perky Delia Templeton.

She stopped at the desk on her way out to schedule the appointments and pay her bill, thanking her lucky stars that Sean McAdams had always provided decent health insurance for his employees at Angel River.

She'd already told Johnnie at Crossing West that she wasn't going to be able to make it there that afternoon, but the doctor's appointment had actually taken less time than she'd expected.

So she drove back to her motel in Weaver, changed into a pair of old jeans and a sleeveless shirt that snapped down the front and drove over to the horse rescue.

Megan wedged her truck into a narrow space in the round parking lot. As was her practice, she stopped at the front pasture to greet Latitude and the other horses. The Shetland was gone now, adopted out to a family from Idaho. All the original quarter horses and thoroughbreds that had been there the first day Megan had visited the rescue were also gone. Some to individual families. Some to other programs.

Rambo—the Tennessee Walker—remained, however, and though he waited patiently for Lat to nab the peppermint Megan gave him, he didn't waste any time in getting his treat, too.

Unlike Latitude, Rambo didn't race off again as soon as he'd gobbled the sweet. First, he sidled up against the rail, seeming to ignore Megan, though his ears swiveled her way. At the signal, she reached over the fence and ran her palm over his gleaming coat. "Such a good boy," she crooned. "Wish I could take you home with me to Wymon, but you'll have a nice new place up on the mountain."

Rambo shifted and hung his head over her shoulder, almost as if he was hugging her.

She pulled off her cowboy hat and looped her arm beneath his neck to rub his cheek. "You'll be the most popular dude up there," she told him. "I'm handpicking all your stablemates, so I ought to know." So far, she had chosen only eleven other horses from the places she'd visited with Axel Clay, but it was a start.

The distinct sound of a power saw rent the air, and the horse lifted his head and pranced away.

She was no closer to dealing with the problems of her personal life, but she felt better. All from a few minutes breathing the same air as a horse.

The June sun was bright and warm, and she pulled on her straw hat again as she circled around the first two barns to reach the third. All of the med wing doors and windows were open and she walked through, sketching a wave to Johnnie, who was going through her first-time-volunteer spiel with a group of young teenagers.

Now that school was out for the summer, she'd told Megan it was common to have new groups coming out nearly every day of the week.

Burrito was outside in one of the turnouts, mercifully burr-free now. Her ribs, which had stood out so sharply at first, were much less pronounced now, but she still didn't tolerate anyone getting particularly close and Megan knew J.D. was starting to be concerned about her rehabilitation. If the pony couldn't stand people, she stood no chance of being adopted out.

That didn't mean an end to Burrito. J.D. had already said the pony would stay at Crossing West for the rest of her life if necessary.

But even ponies like Burrito needed to feel loved.

So Megan stopped next to her pen and like every other day since she'd begun volunteering at Crossing West, she extended a fresh carrot.

The scrawny pony acted as if she didn't see it at all.

Megan just waited silently. And after a small eternity she was rewarded.

The pony circled around the perimeter of her fenced run and finally reached out her neck to snatch the carrot between her soft lips.

Then she trotted straight back to her far corner, noisily crunching the vegetable and swishing her tail as if to tell Megan to get lost.

"That's quite an example of patience."

Megan whipped off her hat and whirled at the

sound of Nick's voice. Her own voice felt clamped inside her throat.

But Nick wasn't standing anywhere near her and she had a moment's doubt as to whether she was hallucinating. On top of her restless nights, what else did she need?

"Up here."

She looked up and nearly swallowed her tongue.

He was standing on the roof of the med wing barn wearing work boots, cargo shorts and a tool belt.

And that was it.

Nada.

Nothing else.

No hat to shield his head from the sun.

No shirt to protect his tanned, sinewy shoulders, either.

And the heavy tool belt he wore was doing a good job of dragging his shorts almost beyond his hip bones to the point of indecency.

Gone was the urbane-architect look. In its place was sweaty-construction-guy look.

Face it. Nick Ventura is mouthwatering whatever his look.

She lifted the brim of her hat to shield her eyes from the sunlight. Or from him. She wasn't sure which.

"I timed it." He didn't even have to raise his voice because it carried down to her so easily. "A full seven minutes for that pony to take the carrot."

"It took her longer yesterday." Megan's heartbeat

felt heavy and hard inside her chest. "And the day before that. I didn't know you were back."

"Left you a voice-mail message a couple days ago."

She squinted and loosened her grip on the hat; she was practically smashing it. Fortunately, it was a woven straw that easily sprang back into its usual shape. She jammed it on her head and pulled the brim low over her brow. "Guess I missed it."

Not seeming bothered by the pitch of the barn roof, he walked closer to the edge. "You all right?"

Her nerves tightened. "Why wouldn't I be?"

He crouched. Even from this distance, she could see the gleam of sweat across his chest. "I don't know. You just look…"

She hunched her shoulders and folded her arms. "Look *how*?"

"Pissed off," he said after a moment. "And not in your usual sexy, cranky way."

Her jaw dropped. "Go—" She broke off, painfully aware of the volunteers around her, many of whom were kids. "Soak your head!"

In the pen next to her, Burrito suddenly bucked, kicking both her legs out at the round metal fence post, which clanged loudly.

Megan yanked off her hat again and swatted it against her thigh as she stomped into the dim barn, aiming straight for the feed room. "Miserable, annoying…*man*," she muttered. "Sexy, cranky?" What the hell was that supposed to mean?

J.D. didn't even look up from the supply order she

was working on. "Can I take my pick or is there one man in particular you mean?"

Megan yanked the clipboard with the medicine schedule off the peg and slammed it down on the work counter. But the chart blurred and the harder she stared, the worse it got. She sniffed and a fat roll of paper towels appeared next to her.

She tore off one and wiped her nose with it.

"Want to talk about it?"

"Nothing to talk about." She grabbed a bucket of supplements and started to measure it out, only to realize she had the wrong one. Cursing under her breath, she started over.

J.D. set down her pen and silently left the room. She was back in a matter of minutes with a saddle pad in her hand. She dumped it on top of the medicine chart. "Go."

"What?"

"You don't need to work this afternoon. We weren't even expecting you. So go. Take Rambo out for a ride and get whatever you've got stuck in your craw out of your system."

Stung, Megan started to object. But something in J.D.'s eyes reminded her so much of Rory. "I'm having a b—" She broke off when Johnnie crowded into the room, too.

"Bad day?" J.D. asked. But it wasn't quite a question.

And it was so much better than what had been on the tip of her tongue.

Baby.

She snatched the saddle pad and escaped.

She collected the rest of her tack in the barn next door and within a matter of minutes, was up on the big black horse.

She followed the usual path she took for a pleasure ride. Back around the barns, past the stacks of lumber waiting to be turned into Stan and Susan's private house, then down into a shallow ravine that ran for miles before eventually intersecting a swift-running creek.

As soon as she reached the lumber stacks, though, she could see the house framing was already under way, thanks to the small crew of carpenters currently sprawled in the grass nearby taking a break.

In just a day, nothing at all had become something of form and substance.

And she could see, too, why Nick had been up on the roof of the barn—because it allowed a nearly perfect bird's-eye view of the dwelling.

"At least he could wear a shirt," she grumbled under her breath as she coaxed Rambo to pick up the pace.

The horse responded to her slightest cue and soon she'd left the workers behind and was following the narrow ribbon of water glittering at the base of the ravine.

She rode for at least two hours before she finally decided to stop. She slid out of the saddle, and while Rambo nudged around in the few inches of shallow water, she visited the dark side of a boulder to relieve her bladder, which was the only reason she'd needed to stop in the first place. Rambo, on the other hand, had stamina to spare.

She rejoined the horse standing in the stream and rested her head against him. "You and Earhart would like each other," she told the horse. "She's as pretty as you are handsome."

"Too bad he's gelded, or you could let 'em make babies."

She inhaled sharply, looking around Rambo to see Nick sitting astride Latitude. Her fingers curled against Rambo's soft mane.

It was a testament to how preoccupied she was with her own thoughts that she'd been entirely oblivious to the sound of another horse approaching.

"Rambo's the only company I wanted. How long have you been following us?"

"Long enough, and you're gonna hurt Lat's feelings talking that way."

Latitude was happily picking his way along the streambed, obviously not hurt in the least.

She was glad to see Nick had put on a shirt. But she pulled her gaze from the wedge of his chest still visible beneath the unbuttoned fabric.

"J.D. tells me you want Rambo for the guest ranch."

She lifted her chin. "So?"

He lifted a hand, signaling he meant peace. "So

I think it's a good choice. And I'm a long way from the equine expert that you are."

She eyed him across Rambo's back. Nick hardly looked like an equine anything. Not with the cargo shorts and work boots. Under her watch at Angel River, she'd have never let someone ride wearing boots like that. But at least he was keeping his heels angled down. The last thing she needed was for him to get his foot tangled in a stirrup.

"We're back being suspicious, I see." Latitude stopped to sniff some wildflowers and the leather saddle creaked as Nick crossed his wrists atop the saddle horn. "It'd just be simpler all around if you'd tell me what's happened to get you all worked up since the last time I saw you."

Megan's nerves tightened. "You tell me. You're the one who was gone for the better part of a month."

"Told you on the phone. There was a problem at the job site."

"Must have been one hell of a problem."

"Yeah." His voice was suddenly clipped. "A fore-man was accused of sexual harassment."

She gave him a swift look. "Was he guilty?"

"Yes, she was. And it took all the time I was there to get things straightened out so the victim got what he needed, and my company wouldn't end up get-ting sued."

"But you're the architects."

"And plenty of times have to be the general contractor, as well. All those people on the job site? My hires. Welcome to my world."

"I'm sorry. I didn't know. You didn't say."

"Well, when I was talking to you—on the rare occasion when you actually answered your damn phone—the last thing I wanted to do was waste precious time talking about that!"

She took a moment to absorb that.

"I wasn't worked up," she finally said, not quite through her teeth.

His eyes lightened then, and a sudden smile toyed with the corners of his lips. "You could save all the posturing, sweetheart, and just admit that you missed me."

In answer, she gathered Rambo's reins and swung up into the saddle with her usual ease, only to close her eyes for a moment when the world swayed slightly. She gently adjusted her seat in the saddle and Rambo, already attuned to her slightest cues, set off. When she opened her eyes again, the horizon was once again reassuringly steady.

And she could hear the soft sound of Latitude's hooves and the occasional jangle of his bridle as he followed in their wake.

Megan adamantly resisted the temptation to sneak a peek behind her.

"Did your grandmother like the picture you sent her of you meeting the governor?"

This was what she got for telling Nick all about the Memorial Day dedication. April had taken the photo on her cell phone and forwarded it to Megan, who'd then needed to use the printer at the public library—the old one, not the new one that hadn't opened yet—to print a copy. She'd had to mail it to her grandmother the old-fashioned way since Birdie had neither a cell phone of her own, nor an email account, at least not one that she checked with any sort of regularity.

"She liked it," Megan answered grudgingly.

"Probably enjoyed showing it off to the girls."

She urged Rambo out of the slow-running stream. "Probably." She waved her hand, shooing away a bee, and ducked her head to avoid a low-hanging tree branch. "Did you hear that the park broke a record for the most number of visitors to any of the Wyoming parks that day?" Yellowstone had been higher, of course, but Yellowstone was a national park and a hundred times larger.

"I heard that Ruby's ran out of food in the morning and Colbys ran out of beer that night. Don't think that's happened in the history of Weaver. Ever."

She realized she was smiling and wiped it right off her face. Just because she had a better understanding of Nick's prolonged absence didn't mean everything was all hunky-dory.

She clucked softly and Rambo immediately headed up the sloped bank until the land leveled out again in a panorama of wildflowers and sagebrush.

When Nick didn't say anything else, she did look

back. She blamed the deeply ingrained habit on years of leading trail rides at Angel River.

He was perfectly fine, though, as he surveyed the beautiful scene before them. Despite his claim that he rode only when he had to—so did he *have to* follow her today?—he sat Latitude with the kind of confident ease born of experience.

Megan, who'd been riding most of her life, found riding the former racehorse an exhilarating, somewhat challenging and entirely exhausting endeavor. Which was why she happily left that particular task to J.D., who had a way with the horse like no other.

He caught her watching him and the oddly bemused look he gave her made something inside her chest lurch.

"I've never even seen this spot," he admitted. He looked over his shoulder at the way they'd come. Then to the east. And then the west, where the distinctive summit of Rambling Mountain rose against the sky.

"Bet the sunsets are amazing here." He suddenly shifted in the saddle and Latitude pranced in a sideways circle.

Megan pressed her tongue against her teeth, willing the horse to settle, but Nick didn't turn a hair; he just clucked under his breath to the horse, who shook his beautiful head a few times before lowering it to nuzzle through another patch of wildflowers.

Meanwhile, Nick had his cell phone out and was checking it.

She grimaced. "Girlfriend calling again?"

"If that's a reference to Delia, I've told you. Not my girlfriend. And the only signal out here is GPS."

"There's a loss," she muttered.

"You really *do* hate cell phones."

"They have their uses. Just don't see why people always seem to need to be 'connected' all the damn time."

He looked up as if he was getting his bearings, then back at his screen.

"Why do you care about GPS, anyway?" she asked.

"Curious whose land this is."

"Double-C?" She'd learned the cattle ranch was the most extensive one in the entire region. And that Squire Clay was the patriarch of the family who ran it. A lot of gossip at Ruby's Diner centered on the Clays—particularly the marital discord between Squire and Gloria.

"I don't think so." Nick brought Latitude closer to her and Rambo, holding out his phone for her to see.

She made a face. "What's that?"

"It's a topo map." Latitude took a few more steps in his pursuit of the perfect flower and Nick dismounted. With the reins in hand, he walked back toward Megan. "Come here. I'll show you."

She told herself it was only curiosity that prompted her dismount, as well. It certainly wasn't because she'd gotten hot and bothered watching him lead a twelve-hundred-pound horse through a field of purple wildflowers.

She'd trusted Rambo not to wander when they'd

been down in the ravine, but up here in the open meadow, she was more cautious, so she, too, kept hold of her reins as she peered at Nick's phone.

"There's the mountain. See?" He slid his thumb over the screen, adjusting the position of the map.

"Mmm." She did, but the map didn't hold a lot of interest. Nick, on the other hand…

His nails were short. Clean. But his thumb was nicked with several shallow cuts already on their way to being healed. And she knew, without having to look, that his palms were calloused.

Her skin was practically prickling from the memory of his hands running over her bare flesh.

"—Lazy-B," he said, still sliding the map this way and that, as her mind had wandered.

"Who?"

"The Lazy-B. Lucy's folks' spread. And this is Crossing West—" he scrolled left on the map and enlarged it "—which I believe we left close to an hour ago."

"Are we on Bureau of Land Management land?"

"Possibly. Braden's that way." He squinted into the distance as if envisioning Weaver's sister town. "Lot of public land between here and there."

"Why are you so interested?"

He pressed a key, making the screen on his phone go dark, then slid it into the front pocket of his slouchy cargo shorts.

Megan quickly yanked her gaze upward, only to get lost in his hypnotic gray eyes.

So hypnotic that she didn't offer up even a half-hearted protest when he suddenly slid his arm behind her waist and dragged her close. Right up against those cargo shorts. That hard, ridged abdomen. That spread of warm, sun-kissed chest.

"I'll tell you." His voice was deep. Soft. "After you tell me why you were so pissed off with me."

She was suddenly, exquisitely aware of just how alone they were. Not a soul for miles and miles, except two horses more interested in the wildflowers than anything else.

Tell him. Just tell him the truth. When he learns you're pregnant, he'll hit the trail so fast you won't have to worry about whether or not you're falling for the guy.

His fingers were slowly gliding up her spine. Beneath her shirt.

"Nick—"

He lowered his head. "Yeah?"

"This isn't a good—" She broke off when his lips grazed over hers and heat streaked through her veins. She pressed her hands to his chest, vaguely surprised to realize she'd dropped one of the leather reins. The other was twisted around two of her fingers.

Rambo didn't seem troubled. The rein still had plenty of slack on his end. If anything, he looked bored.

Nick's lips were moving distractingly along her jaw. Roving over her neck, making her forget anything and everything.

"D'you know how many nights I spent in Gillette thinking about you?" His words tickled her ear. "The feel of you?" His hand moved back down her spine, sliding over her rump. Her hip. "The taste of you?"

His hand moved up to her breasts, which were aching for his attention. He tugged on her shirt, and the snaps popped open.

"How many times I woke up hard, wanting nothing more than this…" He dragged the stretchy knit below one nipple and then the other until they sprang free, tight and hard and so sensitive that when he leaned down to take one in his mouth, she nearly came right then and there.

"And this." His voice deepened even more as he ran his hand straight down, sensations shooting through her when he cupped her through her jeans.

She jerked and spun around, intent on escaping what she didn't really want to escape. And when his hands followed her and he pressed himself hard against her rear, she leaned back against him. His mouth found the nape of her neck. Then the point just below her ear that sent ripples streaking down her spine.

"Undo your jeans," he whispered.

She gasped. "You first."

He laughed softly. And did as he was told.

She quickly followed his lead.

When his hand slid down into her panties and beyond, she didn't care if one of Rambo's reins was tangled around her wrist. Didn't care if it was late in the afternoon and they ought to be getting back soon.

She didn't care about anything except Nick's fingers, petting, swirling, delving, and then the hard press of his leg between hers before he filled her, tighter than ever, thanks to their positions and the fact that her jeans were caught around her thighs.

His breath turned rough against her ear… He was panting, praising, urging—

She cried out, straining back against him, holding his hands to her as the pleasure screamed through her, going on and on and on. And when his hands tightened even further, she felt the pulse of him right through to her very soul.

Chapter Twelve

Eventually, they managed to untangle themselves from each other, as well as Rambo's rein, which was still looped around Megan's wrist.

"Good thing he's a patient soul," Nick said. "And that one—" he gestured at Latitude, who'd taken to rolling around in the wildflowers "—is a romantic."

"Mmm-hmm."

Nick wasn't sure he had a solid bone left in him, but he forced himself to stay upright as he eyed Megan's bowed head.

"Something wrong?"

Her thick blond hair swept her shoulders as she shook her head vehemently.

"Megan—" He cupped her shoulder. Squeezed lightly.

She raised her head and gave him a look that was uniquely hers. Full of nerve. Bravado. But layered with a streak of softness that he had already decided was a mile wide.

Not that he intended on pointing that out just now when she'd taken the stuffing out of him and his defenses were low.

"You ripped my panties," she said and pulled the thin white fabric right out from her loosened jeans.

He laughed. "Sweetheart, I'll buy you a dozen pairs to replace 'em."

She pitched them at his head. "I'll buy my own, thanks."

He caught them and shoved them down into one of his many pockets as he watched her start to zip up her pants. When she noticed him watching, color flagged her cheeks and she turned her back on him.

He grinned. "Now I'm just going to be thinking about you going commando."

"Oh, my god," she muttered, yanking her shirt down over her hips. "Cool your jets, would you?"

He grabbed her waist and swung her around to face him, loving the way her eyes went wide and color filled her cheeks. "You're beautiful, you know that?"

Her lips thinned and she looked away. "Cut it out. And get Lat out of the weeds. God only knows how many burrs he's picking up."

He caught her face in his hands and pressed a kiss to her lips. Then another. By the third, she was swaying slightly, a dazed look in her eyes.

Satisfied, he whistled, and the horse immediately rolled to his feet, dancing around like the big puppy that he really was. Nick caught the loose reins and thanked his lucky stars for the horse's goofy nature because J.D. would have strung and quartered him if her beloved Latitude had truly gotten loose.

"Don't see any burrs but he did find a good patch of mud." He unsaddled the horse, shook out the saddle pad, wiped off the mud with his shirt and re-saddled him. "You're gonna need a shower for sure, aren't you, bud?"

"Aren't we all," Megan muttered. She circled around Nick and the horse, giving them both a critical eye.

Then she swung up into her own saddle and turned back in the direction of Crossing West. "Let's just hope everyone's left for the afternoon by the time we get back."

Nick shared the sentiment. He was satisfied with life in Weaver, but that didn't mean it was all that convenient always being surrounded by people getting in your business.

Fortunately, when they plodded past the newly framed house being built for Nick's grandfather, the work crew was gone.

And there wasn't anyone left in the pens with the horses except for J.D., who just sketched a wave in acknowledgment as they passed.

The sun was sinking toward the horizon by the time they finished cleaning the horses and the tack.

"Come back to my place," he said, when Megan climbed behind the wheel of her truck.

She shook her head and stuck the key in the ignition.

He reached into the truck and covered her hand to keep her from turning it. "Why?"

She looked as if she was hunting for a smart remark. But in the end, she just exhaled. "Because it's been a long day and I'm tired."

He let go of her hand, but only to cup her cheek.

Her lashes fluttered and for a moment she seemed to lean into his palm. Before she had a chance to realize it, he stuck his head through the window and kissed her gently. Knowing better than to push too hard, he pulled away, but not before he'd pressed a slow kiss to her forehead, too.

When he pulled back, her eyes were wide and so full of something that it made him hurt inside. "At least give me a call or send a text so I'll know you got to the Cozy Night okay."

Looking choked up, she nodded and turned the key.

He shoved his hands into his pockets as he watched her drive away.

"Want to come in for supper?" J.D. stopped next to him.

He started to shake his head. What he was starving for wasn't going to be found at her dinner table. But the phone suddenly vibrating in his pocket made him nod instead. "Thanks." He pulled out the phone, ignored the notification that Delia was calling and opened up the GPS map. "I want to talk to you and Jake about the land heading north up the ravine. Ten, twelve miles or so."

He was pretty sure he'd found the perfect location to build his home.

How difficult it might be to acquire the land remained to be seen.

But the real challenge, he knew, was going to be convincing Megan that she belonged there with him.

By the time Megan let herself into her motel room, she'd at least managed to stop shaking.

The tears, though?

They kept burning behind her eyes no matter how many times she thought she'd beat them back.

She locked her door, yanked off her clothes and kicked them to a corner.

She'd never be able to wear any of them again without thinking about Nick and what they'd done out in that wildflower meadow.

She stood under the shower until the hot water ran out. And then she still stood there until her skin felt shriveled and cold.

She dried off in front of the mirror, turning this way and that. Studying her reflection. Wondering how she could be so inwardly changed yet not show it at all outwardly. She flattened her palms over her belly.

Was there a slight swell?

The bruise on her leg from Burrito had long faded. But she still sensed fingerprints on her hip. Nick's fingerprints.

Her nipples pebbled and she covered them with her hands.

The shrill ringing of the room's telephone made her jump. She whipped the thin towel around herself as she circled her bed to stare at the thing sitting on her nightstand. The phone looked as old as the one that Birdie had.

Not once in all the time that Megan had been at the Cozy Night had she ever used it.

She gingerly lifted the receiver. "Hello?"

"Finally!" Rory's voice sounded loud and Megan held the phone out a little. "I was starting to get the feeling you've been avoiding me!"

Megan sank down on the bed. *The* bed. She hopped up again and switched to the other one. She couldn't go far. The coiled phone cord made sure of that. "I haven't been avoiding you. You're the one globe-trotting all over with Mr. Richie Rich. Where were you the last time you left me a message? Somewhere in Maine?"

Rory laughed. "Okay, okay. Point taken. So how *are* you? Gage tells me that things are coming along great with the lodge on Rambling Mountain."

Megan swiped her wet hair off her shoulder and tightened the towel around her breasts. "Coming along," she agreed.

"Everything working out with the new architect?"

She chewed the inside of her cheek. "That's one way to put it."

"Gage is pretty impressed with Nick Ventura. Says he would have wanted him on the job from the beginning except he wasn't available at the time."

She stopped chewing her cheek and started picking at a cuticle. "He managed to get available well enough after Chance Michaels bowed out. How's Killy?"

"He's great. We dropped him off at Angel River after the school year finished. He's spending the month with my dad. Of course, to Gage's chagrin, all he could talk about was getting to see Noah again."

To Megan's thinking, Gage's younger brother was finally getting his footing after a rocky start when he'd first come to the ranch with Gage last year. Now he was a regular part of the staff there, pitching in on everything from housekeeping to entertaining the guests with his piano playing. "Noah's not so bad," she said. "He's stuck with things pretty well since you guys left." She lay back on her bed. "Still hasn't cut off the man bun, but he's cute as hell and the guests like him."

"But you and he never—"

"God, no!" Gage's half brother was even younger than Nick. She threw her arm over her eyes but that did nothing to eradicate Nick's image from the backs of her eyelids. He made Noah seem like a schoolboy in comparison.

"Well, you talked about it once upon a time if you'll recall."

"Only to egg you on where his big brother, Gage, was concerned. Besides, Man Bun is all about his girlfriend, Marni, anyway." She lowered her arm and rolled onto her side, stuffing a pillow under her cheek. It was so easy to fall back on the easy subjects of conversation. And put off the not-so-easy one. "She moved into his cabin even. Surprised you haven't heard."

"Things are better between Gage and Noah, but they've still got a long row to hoe."

"No more talk from your dad about selling Angel River?"

"Not now. For one thing, business has still been increasing since last fall. And for another, Gage is making an investment there so Dad can do some of those upgrades we'd been putting off for too long."

Megan couldn't help teasing. "My, my, my... How a little thing like falling in love can bring about huge changes." Less than a year ago, Rory had feared that Gage intended to buy out the ranch altogether.

Rory laughed again. "Well, speaking of changes..." She hesitated.

And Megan instinctively knew what was coming next.

"You're going to have another godchild! I'm due the end of January!"

Megan closed her eyes, exhaling carefully. She was due the beginning of December.

"Well? Hello? Have you passed out in shock?"

"No." Her throat felt tight. "That's great. I always

said you make good babies. Just look at Killy. He's probably over the moon with the idea of being a big brother."

"We actually haven't told him yet. I mean, it's still so early yet. We'll wait until we pick him up from Angel River next month." Rory's joy was bubbling over in her voice. "I've been trying to tell you for weeks now! Ever since I found out. You were the first one I wanted to tell…well, after Gage, I mean."

There'd been a day when Rory would have told Megan everything first.

"I'm glad for you," Megan said quietly. Sincerely. "You and Killy finally have the kind of family in Gage that you deserve."

"Talking about family, I think Gage is actually softening where Vivian Templeton is concerned."

The less Megan heard the Templetons mentioned, the better, but Rory wasn't to know that. "Is he going to tell her that she's his long-lost grandmother, after all?"

"He's not quite at that point yet. But I think he will be. I think he's realizing that even though his father was estranged from Vivian before he died it doesn't have to mean that Gage should be, too. As far as Vivian Templeton knows, her son died alone as a young man. She never even knew about Thatcher's life with Althea Stanton or that they'd had a baby together."

"The positive influence of Rory McAdams—who believes family trumps all—strikes again."

Rory laughed softly. "That's Rory Stanton to you,

my friend. You were the one who knew all along I'd end up with Gage."

For some damn reason, Megan was tearing up again. "When something is so obvious, it's obvious." She cleared her throat. "You know after a month at Angel River, Killy's gonna want a man bun again like Noah's."

Rory laughed. "You think he doesn't have one already? Anyway, Gage is waving at me that we're late for our dinner reservations, so I'll let you go. Next time you have a spiked hot chocolate, add an extra shot of Irish cream for me, okay? It's going to be a while now before I get to indulge."

"Next time," Megan promised huskily.

"Love you!"

"Love you, too," she replied but Rory had already hung up.

Megan dropped the receiver onto the hook and flopped back on the bed. "By the way," she said to nobody. "You're going to be a godmother, too."

Then she groaned and pulled the pillow over her head.

The next morning, Megan drove up the mountain as usual, bracing herself all the while to face Nick again.

He wasn't there.

She told herself she was relieved. It meant she could study the latest horse listings Axel had sent her in peace and quiet.

Well. Not so much peace, since there was a constant stream of carpenters coming and going from the trailer. And definitely not so much quiet, since there were cement trucks coming and going with almost as much frequency as the carpenters, as the foundations for the stables were completed.

But she stuck it out until it was nearly lunchtime and then she drove back down the mountain. Again. Like usual.

There was an empty stool at the counter next to Dori, and Megan slid into it quickly because if she didn't, she knew she could be in for a wait.

"Hi, there, sweetie." Dori reached over the counter for the coffee carafe and refilled her cup. "You're looking peaky. Heard you had an ulcer. Is it kicking up?"

Once a liar...

"I don't have an ulcer," Megan said sharply. Then, taking note of Dori's expression, she managed a smile. "Not—not anymore," she added in a much nicer tone.

Dori's stricken look immediately lifted, and she patted Megan's arm in a comforting manner. "That's a good thing. I had a cousin once who had stomach troubles all her life. Took an autopsy for the doctors to realize that's what did her in." She poured an outrageous amount of sugar into her coffee. "Foolish girl never would trust a doctor while she was alive."

Tina set a tall glass of lemonade in front of Megan. "The usual for you, Megan?"

"BLT."

"Changing it up from the Reuben, eh?" She winked and tore the little page off her order pad to stick it on the revolving ticket holder in the kitchen pass-through.

"Variety is the spice of life," Megan told her.

"That's what I keep telling Howard," Dori said, "every time he proposes and I tell him no. Variety is the spice of life."

Tina laughed as she added crackers to a tray of soup bowls. "How much variety are you actually having, Dori?"

"Just never you mind," Dori said, bobbing her head.

Megan hid her smile behind her glass of lemonade.

"Well, the only variety I care about right now are the new clothes they've gotten in at Classic Charms," Tina said. She propped her hand on her hip. "I've got a date Friday night."

"With?"

"Eli Scalise."

Dori pointed at Tina with her coffee mug. "If you think dating the sheriff's son is going to get you out of those parking tickets, you're bound for disappointment."

Megan set down her lemonade. "Where's he taking you, Tina?"

"Pizza Bella. It's across town."

Naturally, she couldn't get through a simple lunch without another reminder of Nick.

"I've had their pizza," she said and slipped off the stool. "I'll be right back."

"Your seat is safe with me," Dori promised.

Only it wasn't. Not really. Because when Megan came out of the ladies' room, Nick was sitting there in her spot, his back to the counter.

He was nodding at something Dori was saying, but it was obvious that he was waiting for Megan.

Considering her absolute lack of control during their encounter the day before, it was probably just as well they were surrounded by Weaver's finest diner afficionados and gossips to keep her on her best behavior.

She suppressed the urge to cut and run, and went back to the counter. "How'd you know I was here?"

"Saw your truck parked out front."

Megan started to cross her arms but pushed her hands into her pockets instead. "The foundations are going in for the stables." Though he probably knew that as well as she did. "How long before they can start framing?"

"By Monday."

She chewed the inside of her cheek. Once the building began in earnest, her remaining days in Weaver would be numbered. She ought to be glad of that. Glad to be going home where she belonged.

"BLT's up, Megan." Tina set the basket on the counter behind Nick.

"Can you pack it to go?"

"Sure." Tina swept away the basket again without batting an eye.

"Have plans this afternoon?"

"Beyond my BLT?" And having to pee every time

she turned around? Not that she intended to tell him *that*. "There are a couple horses Axel told me about that I want to see. Owned by Evan Taggart."

"He's the vet."

"So I've heard."

"You can see Evan's horses anytime."

"Maybe I don't want to see Evan's horses anytime," she said mildly. "I've already put in the prefab order. Is there something else you need me to do?"

The smile that started in his eyes made her feel hot inside. She took the white paper sack that Tina held out over Nick's shoulder, trying not to touch him, but it was pretty futile considering how crowded the diner was and how closely situated the counter stools were.

She felt his fingers brush her hip and she quickly moved away to the end of the counter, where the cash register was located. She gave enough cash to cover the bill and a tip before sidling her way through the line of people waiting for a seat.

Nick was on her heels.

"This place is always busy for lunch, but this is really bad," he said.

"Blame the people wanting to visit Lambert State Park." Megan crossed the sidewalk toward her truck.

He made a sound and caught her arm. "What's the rush?"

She looked pointedly at his hand.

His lips tightened slightly. "Don't tell me that we're going back to square one, Megan."

"Maybe I don't want to be the next lunchtime topic

for that group in there." She jerked her head at the restaurant behind them and continued toward her truck.

He snorted softly. "It wouldn't matter if we stood ten feet apart and never made eye contact when it comes to town gossip. If they think it'll make a good story, they'll still have us getting *nekkid*—which is a helluva lot more scandalous than just plain old *naked*—and then they'll toss in a few wild monkeys and a jealous ex for good measure."

"Well, shoot. I've always preferred keeping my wild monkeys under wraps." She yanked open the truck door and tossed her sandwich inside on the seat. "As for the jealous ex, that'd be your domain."

"I don't have a jealous ex."

She felt certain he had a jealous Delia waiting in the wings, though.

But she didn't say that. "Don't you have work to do this afternoon? Architect stuff or carpenter stuff or—or something?"

"I cleared my schedule, actually."

"Why?"

"Because it's a sunny June day." He lifted his arms. "And I thought maybe you'd like to take a ride out to Lambert Lake."

"Nick—"

"Come on, sweetheart. You know you want to."

That was the problem. She did.

"I'm not going swimming," she said flatly. "I don't even have a swimsuit."

"As appealing as skinny-dipping with you would

be, there are more private swimming holes than Lambert Lake for that." His eyes twinkled. "We can borrow a horse trailer from Crossing West. And god knows J.D. has plenty of horses to ride."

She could feel herself weakening and knew that he could see it, too.

"Go back to your motel and change," he said. "I'll meet you there."

Before she could summon an argument—any argument—he was already gone, striding confidently along the sidewalk toward his SUV parked down the block.

She was pretty sure he was actually whistling, too.

She realized she was smiling, and she huffed out a breath and got behind the wheel.

"What kind of a guy whistles when he walks?"

One who is too good to be true?

She met her eyes in the rearview mirror as she waited to back out into the midway traffic.

Or one who actually is *that good?*

Either way, she couldn't see how things between them could possibly end well.

But end, they would.

For Forrester women, they always did.

Chapter Thirteen

But they didn't end just yet.

Because June slid into July, passing in an almost frenzied haze of activity. Megan was often on the mountain watching over the construction of the stables, or she was at Crossing West with the rescue horses. And she also spent time tramping through another patch of Lambert State Park with Nick, while she put horses she was selecting for the guest ranch through their paces.

Mostly, it seemed, she was with Nick.

And the longer that went on, the harder it got pretending she hadn't waded way into the deep end without a life preserver. The longer she went without telling him her secret, the harder it got to break her silence. She was even avoiding Rory's phone messages now. Talking to Rory would be like opening up a door to Megan's conscience.

And Megan's conscience had enough on its hands.

Particularly now that she really did have *two* beds in room number 22 that she couldn't sleep on without remembering their lovemaking.

She probably should have just succumbed to his frequent suggestions to stay at his place. But on that one point, at least, she'd managed to hold firm.

Because it was a very solid reminder that her stay in Weaver was only supposed to be temporary.

And by the time July rolled around and the Independence Day bunting started showing up on every storefront in town, Megan's stay was supposed to be coming to an end.

Just in time, too, she realized, when she got up the day before Nick's library was set to open and her jeans flat-out wouldn't button.

In fact, she couldn't even get the zipper up past the halfway mark.

She dragged off her jeans and went to stand in front of the bathroom mirror. When she looked at her reflection straight on, nothing about her figure seemed the least bit different.

But when she turned sideways…

"Holy—" Her jaw dropped and her hands moved down over the perfectly obvious swell. "You've sure picked your moment to make an appearance." Megan was supposed to be meeting Nick at the library to help set up for the grand opening the next day. Which meant she needed to be wearing something other than a nightshirt!

She went through every piece of clothing she'd brought with her from Angel River, trying to find something that would fasten. Which was a monumental failure. She was feeling a little desperate when she finally settled on layering two of her longest shirts—one buttoned and one not—over her half-zipped jeans.

When she walked into Classic Charms a half hour later—having had to wait for the place to even open for the day—she felt like every eye she passed could see her for what she was.

Pregnant lady walking.

When the clerk opened the door, Megan aimed straight past the eclectic selection of antiques and bric-a-brac they sold for the clothing in the back. Ninety-nine percent of what Megan wore were clothes fit for dealing with horses. She wore jeans, jeans and more jeans. She wore Western-cut shirts because that's what she'd always worn. The only time she ever dressed up was when some event at Angel River—like a wedding—required it.

All of which meant that she couldn't just flip through a few hangers to find what she knew and felt comfortable in.

She finally just grabbed a pair of jeans an entire size up from her usual, and the only two blouses she could find that didn't cling or possess freaking *ruffles*.

She left the store wearing the jeans and the least

colorful of the two blouses and drove straight to the library.

Nick was already there, as were Lucy and Beck and several others. Fortunately, none of them seemed to notice anything was different about her at all.

She helped arrange the tables for the breakfast that would be provided the following morning and lined up dozens of pretty white chairs that reminded her of the ones they used at Angel River for weddings.

And she tried not to look as annoyed as she felt when Delia Templeton showed up in her short shorts and her skintight red, white and blue top and her little clipboard with the daisy stickers on the back.

Megan knew the other woman was deeply involved in the grand opening, but seriously. Did that mean she had to stand so close to Nick while they reviewed whatever important notes were on her daisy clipboard?

"A gnat couldn't get between them," she muttered as she repositioned a chair for about the tenth time.

"What's that?" Gloria Clay was tying blue bows onto the back of every other chair.

"Nothing." Megan quickly scooted the chair where it belonged.

But it was as if the older woman knew exactly what was bothering her, because Gloria looked at where Nick and Delia were standing near the sliding doors of the library entrance and then back to Megan again.

"Nicky's a good boy," she said.

Megan wanted to choke. There was nothing at all

boyish about Nick. He'd proven that to her time and time again. She made some sound that she hoped the woman took for agreement. "I can help with some of those bows."

Gloria handed her the plastic bin containing the bows. "That's a very becoming blouse," she said. "Like a Monet painting. Makes your skin sort of… glow."

Megan flushed self-consciously. "That's sweat," she said, bluffing. "It's already getting hot out here."

"Yes." Gloria smiled slightly, but there was still concern in her eyes. "And likely to get hotter." Then she squeezed Megan's arm and left her to the bows as she waved to Stan and Susan Ventura, who'd just arrived.

Megan swiped her forehead and blindly continued tying on the bows. After the blue ones came the red ones, which took nearly another hour, but at least by then Delia had finally sashayed her flat-tummied self past the chairs to her grandmother's expensive Rolls-Royce, which had no business being on the streets of a town like Weaver.

Everyone who'd helped set up at the library convened afterward for lunch at Ruby's Diner, where three long tables had been reserved.

"Who'd have thought the day would come when you need a reservation at Ruby's?" Axel Clay said from the end of his table. "And look at the traffic out on Main." He gestured at the windows that overlooked the street. "Ever since Memorial Day it takes twice as long to get anywhere."

"Blame the new park," Tina said, leaning past him to set an enormous pepperoni pizza on the table. "We're looking for two more waitresses to bring on just to handle the load."

"I keep hearing this word, *blame*," Gloria said. "As if the park is becoming a bad thing. It was only a month ago that it was dedicated!"

"Gloria's right," Nick said. He was sitting next to Megan and she had to keep grabbing his wandering hand beneath the table. "Otis Lambert donated that land. He did the right thing finally sharing it with the public. Megan and I have done a lot of exploring out there." His laughing eyes caught hers just as she caught his hand again. "And it's pretty spectacular."

"Something else that's spectacular are the stables," J.D. commented as she surveyed the pizza. "Jake and I took a drive up there the other day to see how it all was looking. The lodge is obviously going to be gorgeous, but I didn't expect the stables to be nearly finished already."

"Only waiting on an order for the stall gates and accessories," Megan said.

"Then it's just a matter of moving the new residents into those stalls," Axel said.

"Have you actually found as many horses as you were hoping to?" Tina set another pizza on the table.

Megan nodded. "Nearly. Have another half dozen to go."

"Bet you can find them at Clay Farms' sale next month."

Megan didn't answer. She would no longer be in Weaver by then. She'd been hoping to have all the selections made before she had to go home. So she could see for herself that they were all settled and happy before turning over the reins to Jed and whomever they hired to take care of the horses after that.

J.D. finally selected a slice of pizza. "When did Bubba put pizza on the menu, anyway?"

"Probably when he found out how much business Pizza Bella was getting," Stan said.

J.D. glanced around their table, ducking her head slightly. "This ain't no Pizza Bella pizza," she said, barely moving her lips.

Bubba's head shot through the pass-through, proving that he had the hearing of a bat. Which was probably why he never missed a nugget of gossip. "What's that you're saying about my pizza?"

"Nothing," J.D. brightly assured him. She held up the droopy slice. "It's great, Bubba."

His head disappeared again, but his voice didn't. "It's crap," he yelled. "And it'll stay crap until I get a decent pizza oven back here."

"Talk to your boss," Axel yelled.

"She's *your* cousin."

Axel considered that for a moment, then nodded. "Makes sense. We want better pizza, we make sure Tabby gets her cook a better pizza oven."

"Doesn't seem to be stopping anyone," Megan

pointed out as Nick nabbed the last two slices with his free hand and dropped one on her plate.

"Amen to that." He grinned and she had to catch his wandering hand yet again.

She angled her head toward him and widened her eyes in a would-you-stop? sort of way. If she weren't afraid his hand would wander up her belly, she would have been squirming for a whole 'nother reason.

Naturally, he didn't stop.

Until she deliberately let her hand do some wandering of its own, which made him blink twice and nearly choke on his bite of pizza when she dragged her fingertip down his fly.

Satisfied that she'd made her point, she left the table to visit the ladies' room. When she returned, she tore off the sagging cheesy portion of her pizza slice to concentrate on the crust, which was her favorite part, anyway.

Nick polished off the piece she'd removed, and then handed her the crust from his slice.

"Oh, my god," J.D. said with a laugh, obviously noticing. "It is love for sure when Nick Ventura voluntarily gives up his pizza crusts."

Megan froze, the crust halfway to her mouth.

"Jeez, J.D." Axel shook his head. "Tactful much?"

Megan glared at Nick. "I thought you never ate them because you didn't *like* them!"

His eyebrows rose. "Did I ever say that?"

"Well, no, but—" She tried handing the crust back

to him. "Here. I don't want yours. I'm satisfied with my own."

"Maybe you don't *want* 'em but maybe I'm satisfied watching you enjoy something from me."

She felt her face flush and wished that she was anywhere other than where she was.

She shoved back her chair. "I gotta go."

"Megan—" Nick caught her hand. "Relax. It's just a pizza crust."

But it wasn't. Not to her. "It's fine," she lied. "See?" She snatched up the crust and shoved half of it in her mouth. "I just, uh, realized how late it's getting." She chewed rapidly around her words. It was hardly polite but she was running on a thin edge of nerves. She managed to swallow the mouthful. "It's Birdie's birthday and I should have called her by now." The birthday part was true. Needing to call her wasn't, because Megan had done so when she'd gotten up that morning.

"I'll stop by later."

"No need. I know you've still got stuff to do this afternoon to get ready for tomorrow's big library unveiling. I'll see you there tomorrow!" She smiled as she backed away from the table, and Nick's family.

The fact that she felt as comfortable with all of them as she did with Rory and Killy was enough to send her toppling off that thin edge.

She bumped a chair behind her and hastily apologized to the middle-aged woman occupying it before she made it out the restaurant door and onto the sidewalk.

That's when she realized her truck was still parked at the library.

"Stupid, stupid, stupid," she muttered.

It wasn't as though the library was miles and miles away. Nothing in Weaver was miles and miles away.

But as an exit strategy, she hadn't thought it out very well.

Can't go forward without taking a first step, missy.

She didn't need Birdie-isms in her head, either.

She blew out a breath and started walking.

He should have gone after her. Right then and there. Not let her run away, whether or not she needed to call her grandmother.

Instead, he'd sat around on his ass at Ruby's because J.D. had advised him to give Megan some space. Some time.

Nick was sick of space. Sick of time.

He'd been giving her both since March and his patience was wearing thin.

It didn't help knowing that the stables up on the mountain were going to be done before their expected completion date.

Megan would have the perfect excuse to run back to Angel River no matter what was happening between the two of them.

He went by the library first, but her truck was already gone. And then, when he finally made it through the damn traffic clogging the small-town road and arrived at the Cozy Night, her truck wasn't there, either.

He wasn't going to think the worst.

Not yet.

Most of her work on the mountain might be nearly complete, but she still had horses to procure and get settled.

No matter how freaked out Megan was about Nick, she wouldn't run out on an opportunity to give more horses a home on the mountain.

The reasoning was sound enough. But the knot in his gut meant he wasn't convinced.

He parked next to the two Harleys taking up the spots in front of Megan's room and got out.

The dull brown curtains didn't quite stretch all the way across the window of her room, and he tried looking through the inch that was left uncovered.

Just to reassure himself that her stuff was still in there.

But no matter which way he tried angling his view, all he could see was the damn window frame or the air-conditioning unit below the window that was rattling and wheezing out hot air against him.

"Are you a Peeping Tom now?"

He jerked around to find Megan, and his relief was so massive it made him mad. "Took you long enough!"

"I needed some space, okay?" She stepped past

him to stick her key in the door lock. "I have...things I need to work out in my head."

"Your head or your heart?"

"You're making the mistake of thinking I have a normal sort of heart."

He barely squelched a snort, realizing she actually believed that. "There's nothing wrong with your heart, Megan."

"Really? You wouldn't say that if you knew—" She broke off and pushed open the door to step inside, but when he tried to follow, she turned and blocked the way.

One hand on the door. One hand on the doorjamb.

He looked from her white knuckles to her face.

"If I knew what, sweetheart?"

Her chin set. "I'm *not* your sweetheart! I don't need you...analyzing me or thinking you know me better than I know myself. And I don't *need* your pizza crusts!" Her voice shook.

The door next to Megan's slammed open and an old man in biker gear stuck out his head. "Everything all right over there? You okay, Meggie? This guy's not bothering you, is he?"

Nick eyed Megan.

Megan, however, was eyeing anything but Nick. "I'm fine, Oscar."

The guy gave Nick the stink eye before withdrawing back into his room.

"Meggie?"

Her gaze finally flicked toward his and then away

again. Her lips were a thin line. *"Nicky?"* Then she huffed noisily and lowered her arms, turning her back on him.

He stepped inside the room after her and shut the door.

She was holding her hair back from her head and it reached halfway down the back of her swirly-colored shirt. "You know I'm older than you?" she suddenly asked. Her voice had steadied again, but she still had a panicky look in her eyes.

He shook his head, trying to follow her unexpected question. "What?"

She dropped her hands and turned. "I am older—" she pointed to herself and spoke slowly, as if he had suddenly lost his grasp on the English language "—than you."

He captured her finger. "Who the hell cares about a couple of years? Or even if it were a dozen years? You're not seriously picking a fight over that."

She pulled away her hand and paced around the bed. "I'm not picking a fight. I'm pointing out a fact."

"Here's a fact." He followed her. "You heard what J.D. said and you freaked out. You don't want to face what's really going on here. What's going on between us."

"There's nothing going on between us except some—" She broke off and moistened her lips. "Some good sex."

He raised his eyebrows. *"Good?"*

"Okay." Her eyes wouldn't meet his. "Very good. Exceptional, maybe. Feel better?"

"I'd feel better when you stop reducing this—" he swept his hand through the air between them "—to some phenomenal sex."

She folded her arms and studied the short, neat nails on her left hand. "I said exceptional. Not phenomenal."

If he wasn't so aggravated with her sheer stubbornness, he would have laughed.

Patience, Nick.

He propped his hands on his hips rather than reach for her and kiss some sense into her.

It took him longer than a simple count of ten to conquer the idea.

"I am in love with you," he finally said, and his flat statement could probably be heard through the thin walls by Oscar. "And you—" he raised his voice over her loud snort "—are falling for me. Things would be a lot easier if you'd just admit it."

Her cheeks were pale, but her eyes were hot. "Forrester women don't fall for men."

"You fall for women, then? 'Cause I gotta tell you, sweetheart, you seem to like what I have to offer pretty well."

She looked like she wanted to slug him and right then he just might have welcomed it.

At least it would be an honest reaction, versus the bull she was trying to peddle.

But her fists uncurled after a moment and she

folded her arms again, probably not even realizing how vulnerable she looked doing it.

"You're not in love with me," she said with a sudden calmness that infuriated him. It was the voice she used when she was working with that scrawny pony out at Crossing West. "You're confusing good—okay, *great*—sex with love."

"Being the immature younger man that I am, right?" he drawled. He shook his head. "That's the biggest load of crap outside of J.D.'s manure pile. I'm twenty-nine, Megan. Not nineteen. I've had great sex with other women and managed not to confuse the two. I—" he slapped his chest, returning the favor of speaking slowly, exaggeratedly "—am in love with you."

Her jaw worked and she looked over his shoulder. At the bed. At the ceiling. "I came here for a couple months, Nick. That's it." Her tone sounded a little less calm. "I have a life and a home in Angel River that I can't wait to get back to. Don't blame me if you're making more out of this little fling than I am."

Little fling. Just sex.

If he believed either was true, he'd chalk it up to experience and offer to fill her gas tank for her drive back to Angel River.

Instead, he hung his head and counted to ten. Again.

"Sweetheart," he finally said, "you are a rotten liar."

Her lips twisted. "Let's just…cut our losses here before—"

"Before what? Before you finally give up this pretense you've got going that you don't need anyone? That you don't want the same things everyone wants?"

"What? Wedding rings and a white picket fence?"

He spread his hands. "What've you got against that?" He held out his palm. "And don't tell me it's not in the Forrester DNA."

Her little cell phone sitting on the nightstand let out a soft bleep and she snatched it up. "Hello?"

"*Now* you answer your phone."

She crossed the room and yanked open the door. "Hi, Birdie! How's your birthday going?"

She laughed merrily at whatever her grandmother said, but she was glaring at Nick. She swept her hand pointedly out the doorway.

"No," she said into the phone. "I'm not doing anything important at all."

"And don't say you don't have the *heart*," he told her softly as he stepped past her. "I know better, Megan."

Then he nudged her shaking hand aside and pulled the door closed after him as he left the room.

Chapter Fourteen

"Okay, what's going on? Why'd you call me Birdie?"

Megan's shaking knees gave out and she collapsed on the bed. "Sorry, Rory. H-how are you?"

"A little worried that you've had a stroke!"

"No. Just—just trying to get rid of s-someone a-at my d-door." She sucked in a shuddering breath.

"Cripes on a cracker. Are you crying?"

Megan swiped her face. "No. Yes. Oh, hell."

"I'm coming over," Rory said flatly.

"Oh, sure," Megan scoffed. "S-see you at t-ten to-night."

"More like ten minutes. We're in Weaver. I left you a message two days ago that we were coming to town today! Gage is finally going to meet Vivian this weekend. We're at Colbys right now with April and Jed Dalloway. Just tell me where you're staying."

Megan told her.

She even managed to hold it more or less together until she heard a knock on her door.

She whipped it open and saw Rory there. And promptly burst into tears.

Rory swore and wrapped her arms around her. "Hey, come on. I know Birdie's okay. I talked to her this morning when I called to wish her happy bir—" She suddenly pulled back and held Megan an arm's length away from her. "Oh. My. God. Are you *pregnant*?"

Megan cried even harder. She sank down on the foot of the bed—*the* bed, site of the activity that had altered her life—and buried her face in her hands.

Rory sat beside her, rubbing her back with one hand and covering her twisted hands with her other. "How'd this happen?"

Megan lifted her head and swiped the moisture from her cheeks again. "The usual way. Boy meets girl. Girl meets boy. Stuff happens and—" she pinched her eyes shut to stave off another wave of tears "—voila. You ought to know how it works by now."

"How far along are you?"

Megan stood and pulled her blouse flat against her belly, showing off the distinct bump. "Seventeen weeks." She could see the shock in Rory's eyes, and she threw herself down on the other bed, staring up at the ceiling. "It's Nick's."

"Nick," Rory repeated slowly. "Wait. Nick *Ventura*? Gage's architect?"

"None other." Megan tried for flippancy and failed. Tears kept leaking from the corners of her eyes. It was like a water main had broken.

"What's he doing?" Rory stood, looking fierce. "Trying to pretend he's not responsible?" She propped her hands on her hips. "We'll see about that!"

"He doesn't know," Megan said wearily. "I haven't told him."

"Why not?"

"Because he's going to think he's got to do something about it!"

"Is that so bad?"

"I don't want him feeling responsible for me!"

"Well, honey. He's responsible for that baby inside you."

"Like Jon acted responsible when he left you pregnant even knowing about Killy?" She felt terrible the second she said it. "I'm sorry." She sat up and caught Rory's hand. "I am *such* a bitch."

"No you're not," Rory said with a sigh. "But if I can get over my ex-husband leaving me flat the way he did, I think it's safe to say that you should be able to get over it, too."

"You're over it because you fell in love with Gage Stanton."

"I'm over it because I had you by my side all that

while! You and Dad and everyone at Angel River. Gage is—" Rory flopped her hands.

"What? Icing on the cake?"

"No. He *is* the cake. This—" she pressed her hand to her belly "—is the icing." She sat down on the second bed opposite Megan, still shaking her head with obvious shock. "I can't believe you're pregnant. That we're actually pregnant together!" Her eyes were searching. "What are you going to do? Does Birdie know?"

"Nobody knows but you. Well, you and the Wymon Women's Clinic. And Dr. Ambrose over in Braden."

"You're not exactly going to be able to keep it under wraps, you know. I mean, as soon as I hugged you, I could tell."

"The baby just popped out today," Megan muttered and told Rory about her mad chase that morning to find some clothes that fit. "Until now, you couldn't even tell a thing. Not even the other night when Nick stayed—" She broke off at the look on her friend's face.

"When Nick stayed…?" Rory stood. "Are you involved with him? Like…actually involved? You, queen of the one-night stands?"

"I can count on one hand the number of those one-night stands," Megan said flatly. "Just because I don't get involved, doesn't mean I'm a strumpet."

Rory pressed her lips together. But the sudden twinkle in her eye wouldn't be denied. "Strumpet? Are you going to hate me forever if I tell you how much you sounded like Birdie just now?" She sat down beside Megan. "Of course you're not. And you're the one who's always claimed that men only had one good use. Your words, girlfriend, not mine."

Knowing it was true didn't make it any easier to swallow. "I'm not involved with Nick."

"Well, let's see." Rory held up her hand. "You got here less than two months ago so *obviously* you cooked up that little bun in your oven when you were here back in March." She held up one finger. "Now you're here again, working with the guy—" She paused. "I bet *that* was quite the little surprise."

Megan grimaced. "I can't even tell you."

"Yeah," Rory said tartly. "You *didn't* tell me, which I'm going to make you pay for somewhere down the line." She held up a second finger. "So you've been working with him for weeks now on the barn design, and by the way, Gage and I drove up there earlier today and it's *fantastic,* and now—" she held up a third finger "—it seems he's perhaps *stayed* the night with you? More than once?"

Megan made a face and didn't answer.

Another finger popped up. Rory raised her eyebrows. And still Megan didn't respond. Another finger. And another.

"Fine," Megan said, flopping her arms. "We've been sleeping together for—for a while."

"And yet you say you're not involved." Rory made a soft sound. "Hmm. Very interesting."

Megan glared. "I'm glad you're enjoying yourself so much."

Rory smiled gently. "Oh, Megan. I love you to pieces. It's just so refreshing to know you're finally letting yourself be human like the rest of us." She gave a huge sigh. "So does Nick think he's involved with you?"

Megan pressed her lips together. She pushed off the bedside and went to the window unit, poking at the buttons for the air conditioner, which were about as useless as the buttons for the heat. "He gives me his pizza crusts," she grumbled.

"Oh, dear god, what a fiend."

Megan grimaced. "He claims he's in love with me." She shot a look at Rory when she made a gleeful sound.

Her friend had clapped her hand over her mouth.

"Get control of yourself."

Rory's eyes were dancing. "Sorry." Though she clearly wasn't. "Are you in love with him?"

"How can I be in love?" Just saying the words made her hot and itchy. "I've only known the man a matter of months."

"Do you doubt that Gage and I are really in love with each other? Good grief, you've known Nick twice as long as I knew Gage when I ran after him to Denver."

"Of course I don't doubt it." She jabbed a button so hard it stuck and the unit vibrated more loudly than ever.

"Is that thing going to take flight?"

"I don't know. Maybe." She thumped the side of it with her palm but gave up.

"Megan, whether you love Nick or you don't, you *have* to tell him."

"I know." She clasped her hands behind her neck and squeezed. "It's the right thing to do. I *know.*"

"What are you so afraid of?"

Her eyes suddenly filled again. How could she explain that it was easier to stand on her own when standing on her own was all she'd ever known? "That he's not going to forgive me?"

"For not telling him sooner?"

"Yes. No. Maybe. For getting pregnant in the first place! I don't know."

"First of all, you didn't get pregnant on your own. And maybe he will be shocked. Or freaked out or angry. How'd you feel when you realized you were pregnant?"

"Shocked. Upset." She slid her jaw back and forth. "Freaked out."

"Then you should have some sympathy for the guy."

Megan heaved out a sigh. "I don't know anything about being in a relationship!"

"You don't know much about being a mommy, either," Rory said dryly, "but nature's going to take care of that pretty darn quick. Just like it did with me when I had Killy."

Megan went over to the sink and dried her face on

the hand towel. In the mirror, her eyes were red. Her cheeks blotchy. She started to turn away but snatched up the little jar of face cream. "You know this stuff doesn't work for diddly-squat." She tossed it toward Rory, who caught it. "These lines?" She touched her face beside her eyes. "Still there."

"You have no idea, do you?" Rory set aside the jar and joined Megan. "You—" she pushed Megan around until she was facing the mirror again "—are every woman's worst fear. A tall, beautiful blonde with legs up to here who doesn't have a clue about how gorgeous she is *and* who doesn't even know what it's like to have to count calories so you can fit into your jeans. You're like Gisele Bündchen in cowboy boots!"

"I *can't* fit into my jeans," Megan groused. "I had to buy a bigger pair. Not to mention this foofy blouse."

"Because you're pregnant, doofus! If you don't like the foofy blouse, buy a dress! They're more comfortable, anyway. And the lines?" Rory stretched up on her toes to peer into Megan's face. "Only ones I see are in your mind!"

Megan leaned closer to the mirror. "I see crow's-feet," she muttered.

"I see stress," Rory countered bluntly. "Which happens when you're sleeping with a guy you just might be in love with but haven't told you're pregnant with his baby!"

"Well, jeez," Megan said sarcastically. "When you put it like that…"

Rory threw her arms around her in a tight hug. "Oh, Megan. Just be honest with the guy. If he's worthy of you—and I have the feeling he could be if he's managed to get past *your* defenses—things might just work out beyond your wildest dreams. Look at me. Cake *and* icing."

Megan sniffed and propped her chin on Rory's head. "I've really missed you."

"I've missed you, too, you giant nitwit." Rory straightened and swiped her own cheek. "Now, go. Find Nick and make this right."

"Now?"

"I'm going to say to you the same thing my dad said to me before I went after Gage. You think the world is going to wait on you?" She patted Megan's belly. "Especially now?"

Regardless of Rory's encouragement, Megan felt like a wreck as she drove through town trying to find Nick. She didn't know if the steady stream of traffic made things better or worse for her state of mind.

She went to his condo. His office.

Both empty.

She went to the library.

Also empty except for the festively decorated chairs and tables prepped and waiting for the following day.

The parking lot at Colbys Bar & Grill was full of vehicles jammed every which way. But she didn't see Nick's SUV.

Eventually she pulled into the lot behind Ruby's Diner, which was only empty because the place was closed. She took out her phone and dialed. No doubt Nick would have plenty to say about her finally using it as it was meant to be used.

But he didn't answer when she called. And when the beep sounded to leave a message, she ended the call and threw down the phone, chickening out.

Worrying is a waste of good energy.

"Birdie, get out of my head."

She picked the phone back up. Dialed again. And when the beep sounded, she gritted her teeth. "It's Megan." Brilliant. "I'm, uh—" She jerked when someone knocked on her passenger window and looked over to see Bubba staring in at her. "I need to talk to you," she said hurriedly. "It's—it's important," she said and hung up again. She pressed the button to lower the window.

"You all right?" Bubba's eyes swept over her. He looked more like a beefy bouncer from a biker bar than he did a hometown diner cook. "We closed up more 'n an hour ago."

"I know. I just—" She held up her phone. "Trying to find Nick."

"Oh." He nodded sagely. "Yeah. He's out at Miz Templeton's place."

Megan stiffened. "Delia—"

"Her granny. Vivian."

Megan felt some of the tension leave her. Nick had driven her past Vivian Templeton's oddly palatial estate during one of their afternoons spent at Lambert Lake. She peered at Bubba. "Are you sure? How do you know?"

"After you skedaddled outta the diner earlier, I heard him saying he had a meeting with her this afternoon."

Of course. Bubba of the bat ears.

"Anyway, I was s'posed to take her some of my quiche she likes, and I asked him if he could drop it off for me 'cause there was no way we were gonna be able to close the diner on time. Too many customers."

Would Nick have gone to his meeting after their argument at the Cozy Night?

Of course. The guy never missed an appointment.

"Thanks, Bubba. You have a good holiday tomorrow."

"Will do. Nothing like Independence Day in Weaver."

Megan waited while he crossed in front of her to dump the garbage bags he was carrying in the trash, and then drove out of the lot.

She was glad she only had to make a right turn into the slow stream of bumper-to-bumper traffic. If she'd needed to go in the other direction, she wasn't sure how long it would have taken.

If this was what Weaver had to look forward to until the excitement over the new state park died down, the town definitely needed to get another traffic light or two put up.

It took nearly thirty minutes just to travel the few

miles to the town limits, where the single-lane road widened into the two-lane highway again.

But she wasn't worried about missing the turnoff to Vivian Templeton's place. The multistoried mansion stood out like a sore thumb in a community dominated by simple cattle ranches.

The driveway up to the house was paved in bricks and something inside her lurched when she saw Nick's SUV parked near one of the wings.

She blew out a long breath and climbed from her vehicle, running her hands nervously down the front of her blouse. It had been weeks now since she'd had any bouts with morning sickness and now was not a good time for it to start up again.

Squaring her shoulders, she marched to the massive front door, grasped the enormous door knocker and let it fall a couple times against the wood. She had some serious doubts that it would even be heard, but only a half-dozen heartbeats pounded in her head before the door slowly opened on a tall, bald guy in a suit and weird scarf.

Megan smiled nervously. "Hi. I'm Megan Forrester. I was looking for Nick. Nick Ventura."

The man inclined his head slightly, looking bored. "Come in," he said and turned on his heel. "This way."

She felt seriously underdressed as she followed him through the fancy house. He led her into a two-storied atrium filled with plants. Two staircases on opposite sides of the room ran up to the second level.

He touched the filigreed handrail of the nearest one. "Mr. Ventura is in Mrs. Templeton's office. At the top of the stairs," he intoned.

Megan had the strangest feeling she ought to curtsy and wondered a little hysterically how the guy would react if Killy had been here running up and down the stairs. Her godson *was* Vivian Templeton's step-great-grandson. Not that the woman knew that, yet. "Thank you."

He tilted his head slightly, and Megan swallowed as she started up the stairs. She was already having misgivings. She could have waited for Nick outside and *not* interrupted a meeting with—from the looks of it—his wealthiest client.

She stopped on the third step and turned around. "I think I'll wait," she said to the…whatever he was. Butler? She started back down the stairs but heard a distinctive trill of laughter from above.

She looked up. And saw Delia Templeton standing there alongside Nick and a silver-haired woman who could only be Vivian.

Megan grimaced and darted down the stairs unnoticed by the trio above, hurrying past the butler as she retraced her steps back to the massive door.

She slid around it and made a beeline for her truck. But she hesitated when she went to turn the key in the ignition. Was she a coward or was she a Forrester?

She got out of the truck and leaned against the hood to wait. Sooner or later, Nick would come out.

She wished she'd done more than brush her hair and wash her face before she'd left her motel room.

Like what? Slather on the face cream?

If only she could turn off her brain. She closed her eyes, hauling in a long, deep breath. *Find a little Zen, Megan.*

She exhaled a long, slow breath. Opened her eyes. Lifted her head.

The massive door was open.

Nick was standing on the doorstep.

His mouth was plastered to Delia's.

Megan stared and the world seemed to halt. No birds sang. No insects buzzed. The clouds in the sky stopped drifting and the stupid hope she'd let bloom inside her shriveled.

When something seems too good to be true, it usually is.

Jerking from her stupor, she got behind the wheel and slammed the truck door. She turned the key so hard, she ground the engine before she got it in gear and sped away from the house, her tires vibrating on the herringbone bricks.

She made it back to the motel without even remembering the drive. But the sight of the beds made her stomach churn. Even though she knew it was futile, she went to the office to ask if she could change rooms.

The teenage clerk shook his head. "Sorry. No vacancies. The holiday's got every place in town booked."

She got back in the truck and started driving. She had no clear plan where, but just knew that if she didn't keep moving, she was going to close her eyes and see the image of Delia's hands clenched in Nick's hair. Of his hands on her shapely hips.

She supposed it wasn't surprising that she ended up at Crossing West. With no desire to run into anyone, she drove beyond the big house and parked near the med wing. The place was quiet as a tomb.

Everybody was off for the holiday weekend.

Which suited Megan just fine.

She got a carrot from the fridge in the feed room and went out to find Burrito. The pony was in one of the grassy turnouts. She gave Megan her usual disinterested look before she kicked her back foot.

Maybe it was Megan's wishful thinking that the kick was less fierce than usual.

At least it didn't connect with anything but air.

She sat down on the grass and extended the carrot through the fence. The pony turned her back and swished her tail. "Maybe you and I *are* alike." She leaned her head against the metal pipe. It was warm from the late-afternoon sun. "Too prickly to stand a chance." She waggled the carrot. "What am I going to do now, Burrito? Have any ideas? No?" She let the carrot droop. "Me, either."

She set the carrot in the grass and withdrew her hand. Then she lay down, cradling her arm on her head as she studied the animal. "If you'd just give a little bit, you could have a nice place up on the mountain. One day there will be a lot of kids there. Families who come to spend a week at a guest ranch. Kids love ponies like you. And you don't have to worry about getting too attached to anyone. You'll know better because guests always leave."

Her phone vibrated annoyingly in her pocket and she pulled it out. Stared at the number on the display. Nick's number.

She waited until it stopped ringing. Then she dialed.

Her grandmother answered on the second ring.

"Two calls in one day," she said. "Quite the birthday present."

"Well, here's another present, Birdie. I'm pregnant."

Her grandmother was silent.

"Well? Don't you have any comment at all?"

"Only been wondering how long it'd take you to tell me."

Megan sat up. "What?"

"Missy, you think you can go to the clinic here in this tiny town and the news won't get back to me? Known all along you got yourself in the family way. But I figured you'd tell me when you were ready. Didn't expect it'd take quite this long, though. Roberta told me after three months."

Megan paced along the fencing. "Well, you don't have to worry that I'll be like my mother. I'm not dumping my baby off on anyone else the way she did."

Birdie snorted then. "Know that, too. You've never been like your mama. Have I ever told you that you were?"

"No, but—"

"You've always been like me," Birdie went on. "You're honest."

Megan flinched.

"And a hard worker. And with the right man, you'll love even harder."

She pinched her eyes, but opened them wide again, trying to banish the images there. "How is *that* like you, Birdie? Who've you ever loved?"

"Your grandfather." Birdie sounded irritated. "Or did you think Roberta just hatched outta nowhere?"

"No, but you never talked about him. Everybody in Wymon knows you never got married."

"'Cause he went off to war and got himself killed first," she snapped. "Maybe your mama would've grown up stronger if she'd have had a proper daddy. Instead Robert never knew about her, and she never knew about him."

"I thought you didn't believe in marriage! All of my life, whenever someone mentioned you being all alone and raising me and needing a husband, you said you wanted nothing of the kind!"

"And I didn't. What's the point in marrying anyone aside from the only boy I ever loved? Spent years when your mama was little having people who figured they knew better 'n me telling me I should get married." She hooted. "Told 'em all what they could do with their notions."

Megan paced back the other way. "Why haven't I heard any of this before?"

Birdie huffed. "For what? Robert was dead long before you were born. Now, are you going back to Angel River soon or what? I got a cradle I'm thinking about refinishing and I need to know when you're gonna be wanting it."

Megan's eyes moistened. Apparently, it had just taken a little case of pregnancy to make up for a lifetime of never crying. "The baby is due in December," she said huskily. "You have plenty of time to finish the cradle."

"Then you'll be back."

She looked down at herself and smoothed her hand over her bump. "I told you I would be." She wasn't sure how Sean would take to his head wrangler having a baby, but when it came time for childcare, she'd figure out some solution. "There's no reason for me to stay here."

"Hmm. Figure that's where your baby daddy is."

Megan choked back a soggy giggle after hearing the term on her grandmother's lips. But then again, she didn't know her grandmother half as well as she thought she did. "He's here."

"And?"

"And nothing." She swallowed hard. "I'll be a Forrester woman just like you, Birdie. Bringing up my baby on my own." And hope that if she had a daughter, she'd be nothing like Roberta.

She heard the distinctive crunch of carrot and looked around, expecting to see that Burrito had picked it up off the ground.

But Nick was standing there holding half of it while the pony stood a foot away from him on the other side of the fence, chewing.

"Baby?" His voice was quiet. His eyes were not.

Her grandmother said something in her ear and Megan managed a sound that must've satisfied Birdie, because she hung up.

Megan slowly pocketed her phone, watching Nick warily. "Did you know I was here?"

"My grandfather saw you drive past the house and called me because he figured I was with you."

Nick had way too many relatives in this town. "Surprised you could tear yourself away from Delia."

"She was kissing me, Megan."

"Didn't look that way to me."

"Didn't look to me like you were pregnant, either," he said flatly. "Is it mine?"

Her fist curled. She lifted her chin. "Yes."

"Were you ever going to tell me? Or just keep laughing behind my back over how oblivious I was?"

"I wasn't laughing!" She curled her hand tightly over the fence rail. "And I knew I needed to tell you, but—"

"But you're a Forrester," he said, his voice still flat. He didn't look at her as the pony stretched out her neck and snatched the rest of the carrot from his fingers. "And you don't need anything or anyone." He wiped his hands together and glanced at her. "Don't worry, Megan. I finally got the message."

Then he turned on his heel and walked away.

Chapter Fifteen

"*W*ell?" Nick stood in front of his father and Lucy, waiting.

After leaving Megan, he'd gone to his folks' place, where for the rest of the day he'd paced up and down the living-room floor. He'd raged. He'd fumed.

He'd told Beck and Lucy about Megan being pregnant.

He'd told them about her infernal independent streak that was two miles too wide.

"Don't you have anything to say?"

He caught the look that Lucy gave Beck. "I think I'll leave this one to you," she said, patting his father's arm. Then she crossed to Nick, kissed his cheek and left the room.

He heard her calling to Shelby and Sunny, who'd

been out in the fenced yard leading Shelby's new horse around on a rope, that it was time to get ready for bed.

"What *do* you want me to say, Nick?"

Nick raked his fingers through his hair. "How the hell do I know? She's pregnant, Dad! And she didn't tell me."

"From what you've told me about her, are you really surprised she needed some time before she did?"

"*Some* time? She got pregnant in *March*. It's freaking July. Just because *she* grew up without a dad doesn't mean our child needs to. She should have trusted me. She should have been honest." He threw himself down onto a chair. "Explain that to me, because I'm at a loss."

Beck sighed and perched on the chair opposite him. When they heard Shelby and Sunny tromping up the stairs, he looked in their direction and smiled slightly. "Not everybody finds honesty as easy as you."

He spread his hands, looking down at his palms. "I've loved two women in my life, son. Your mother and Lucy. Harmony gave me you and Shelby. Lucy gave me Sunny. And the one thing I learned after we lost your mom and I met Lucy was that time marches on. It marches on whether you have someone you love by your side or not. And I'm here to tell you, it's a lot better with someone you love. So the only thing I really have to say is actually a question. Do you love Megan or don't you?"

"Yes, I love her. I want to strangle her at the moment, but yeah. I've known it for a while now." He scraped his hand down his face. "But what good is it if she won't trust me?"

"I've never really told you much about my childhood," Beck said. "It wasn't…great." He shook his head and sighed. "But I met your mom. And she loved me despite myself. It took that—meeting her. Loving her. It took all of it for me to learn how to trust. Maybe it'll take you loving Megan for her to learn the same thing."

"She thinks I was kissing Delia Templeton," Nick admitted. "I don't think trust has a snowball's chance in hell now."

Beck's eyebrows rose slightly. "Were you kissing Delia Templeton?"

Nick shoved off the chair. "No. Well, yeah, there was a kiss but not because *I* initiated it."

"Did you stop it?"

He swore. "Of course I stopped it!" He paced across the living room and back again. "I was at Vivian's and Delia just threw herself at me. Right outta the clear blue sky. She's always been flirty, you know, but—" He shook his head. "Next thing I know, Megan's tearing outta there in her truck like the devil's on her heels." He clawed his fingers through his hair again. "Thing is, Megan's the one who said I should've told Delia flat out that I wasn't interested in her that way."

"Probably," Beck said mildly. "But why didn't you?"

Nick grimaced. "I've known her a long time. I thought if I just ignored it, she'd get the message. I didn't particularly want to hurt her feelings. Which I ended up doing, anyway, when I realized Megan was there."

He picked up the squat glass of whiskey that he'd been nursing for as long as he'd been nursing his anger and finished it off. "I'll be surprised if Delia ever speaks to me again after the way I lit into her, and god only knows how that'll affect my working relationship with Vivian."

"I wouldn't worry much about that if I were you. Vivian doesn't strike me as a woman who is swayed too much by the opinions of others, including her grandchildren. Do you know why Megan was there?"

"Looking for me," he said wearily. He sat back down. "Montrose said he was showing her the way to Vivian's office, but she changed her mind and decided to wait outside."

"Any chance Delia knew that?"

"And what? Chose to plant one on me for Megan's benefit?"

"It's been pretty apparent to those of us who know you that you've been taken with Megan from the get-go," his dad said dryly. "Delia's not blind. Desperate people do desperate things."

Nick sat forward and rubbed his face. For a day that had started out with such promise, it had turned into a crap fiesta. He pushed to his feet.

"What're you going to do?"

He exhaled and spread his hands. "Find a solution."

Beck smiled. "There you go."

Some solutions, however, were easier than others.

And it shouldn't have come as any real shock that when he went to look for Megan for the second time that day, this time she really was nowhere to be found.

Not the Cozy Night.

The housekeeping cart was sitting outside room 22 when he got there and he looked in to see the usual maid, Chastity, vacuuming the carpet.

The beds were made.

The closet rod was empty.

There were no cowboy boots or sandals on the floor.

"Do you know where she went?" he asked the girl. "Megan?"

"Sorry." Chastity pointed. "She left that, though, along with a nice tip for me. I'm just not sure if she forgot it or what."

He picked up the napkin he'd drawn on that first time they'd gone to Pizza Bella.

"I think she probably just left it behind," he murmured and slipped it into his pocket. "Thanks, Chastity."

The girl bobbed her head and turned on her vacuum again.

Nick left.

He retraced his route from earlier that day, keeping

his eyes peeled for a sign of her truck. He drove from one end of town to the other; he called everyone that he knew who knew her, and nobody had seen her. He even traipsed through the barns himself at Crossing West just to be sure J.D. wasn't mistaken when she insisted that Megan was no longer there.

It was late by the time he gave up. The only other logical place for her to have gone would be home. Back to Angel River. Earlier, he hadn't believed that she'd leave town without seeing everything through up on the mountain.

But that was before she'd seen Delia kissing him.

The problem was half the town would be turning out soon for the library grand opening. Vivian expected him to be there for it.

Or, at least, she had been expecting him.

After the fiasco that afternoon with Delia, Nick wasn't sure about Vivian at all. Regardless of what his dad believed.

No closer to an answer, he finally drove back to his condo.

And there she was.

Sitting on his front steps in the pool of light cast by his porch light.

He closed his eyes, exhaling on a prayer.

He got out of his SUV and slowly approached. "I went looking for you."

Megan rubbed her hands down her thighs and stood.

She'd changed. She wasn't wearing the jeans and

the wildly colorful blouse. Now she was wearing a dress.

He caught himself from shaking his head, not sure that he wasn't seeing things. "I've never seen you in a dress before."

She twitched the skirt, which looked sort of like denim and reached to just above her knees. "I borrowed it from April this afternoon." Her chin came up. "You might as well know. She and Jed know about the baby."

Which meant by now most of the family would know, too.

She tugged at the dress again. "Looks stupid, I know."

"You look beautiful." His throat felt tight. "You always look beautiful. In a hard hat. In jeans. In a dress. In nothing at all." He cleared his throat. "How long have you been sitting here?"

"Two bottles long." She gestured at the empty water bottles sitting on the step and shifted. "I wasn't going to drive around town again looking for you. I figured you had to come back sooner or later."

"You're smarter than me. I drove around town twice today looking for you."

She shifted again and looked away.

He stepped closer. "I wasn't kissing Delia Templeton," he said.

Her lashes swept down. "I know."

"She just— You what?"

"She told me."

He had to shake his head. "It's been a long-ass day here, sweetheart. You're gonna have to catch me up."

"Can I—" She looked around at everything but him. "Can I use your bathroom first? Two bottles of water and—"

He swore and took the stairs in a single step to unlock the door and pull it open. "Go."

She bolted inside for the powder room just off the foyer.

He threw away the water bottles and started to close the front door, but then stopped and left it open. The last thing he wanted to do was spook her by hemming her in.

He leaned against the back of the couch and waited for her to emerge.

She did, just a few minutes later, her cheeks looking flushed. She clasped her hands in front of her. "I should have told you," she said abruptly. "As soon as I realized I was pregnant."

He nodded. "You should have."

She moistened her lips. "And I'm sorry that I didn't."

His dad's words hung in his mind. "Okay."

"And about Delia—"

He lifted his hand. "I don't care about Delia as long as you don't care about Delia."

"But you said to catch you up."

"And I had ninety seconds to rethink that. We'll waste time later talking about how and why she told you the truth. Right now, the focus is you. And me. And nothing else."

Her hand drifted over her abdomen. "I don't expect anything. N-no matter what you said earlier today. I'm capable of—"

"Tough."

"What?"

"I said, tough."

She shifted, giving him a wary look. "I don't understand exactly what that means."

"Then I'll be clearer. It means I expect everything." He pushed away from the couch. "When you first came back here in May, and we went for Chinese, I lied to you, too."

Her eyebrows pulled together.

"I told you I had no expectations. Remember?"

"I remember everything." Her voice was husky.

"Probably the biggest lie I've ever told."

She watched him warily.

"Because I expect *everything*. And I should have told you that back in the beginning when you were pretending that nothing had happened between us. I shouldn't have just left a few messages for you at Angel River and tolerated you ignoring me."

She looked away, her lips set.

"I shouldn't have allowed the time to slip by just because I knew you'd be back. I should have told you that I expected everything where you're concerned."

He lifted her chin until her eyes stopped shying away from his. "I expect your days and your nights.

I expect your strength and your fears. Your laughter and your temper and—" he brushed his thumb over her cheek "—your tears. I expect you to let me love you until there are no days left. Today. Tomorrow." His voice got hoarse. "Always," he croaked. He took a breath. "And I expect you to love me back just as hard. I should have told you all of that. *Before* you even knew about this." He slid his hand down her belly and covered her hand with his. "Because I knew then how I felt about you. And I should have made it very clear, so you'd have time to get used to it. So you wouldn't be so afraid. And so that you would understand and know that there would never be any Delias or anyone else for me as long as there is *you*."

Her eyes flickered. "But the baby—"

"Will grow up with an amazing mother. But this isn't about the baby. It isn't about whether or not you could do motherhood all on your own. Or if I could do fatherhood on my own.

"This is about us. You and me. You don't have to admit you love me yet. You don't even have to agree to marry me yet. Maybe you're not ready to trust your heart, but *I* am."

Her eyes shimmered. "If I get used to you and you leave—"

"Never," he said swiftly. "Megan. I am yours. And you're mine. That's it. That's all. It is set in stone as hard as the granite on Rambling Mountain. The baby?" He pressed his forehead to hers for a moment. "Sweetheart, the baby's just icing on the cake."

Megan sucked in a shaking breath. She stared up at Nick. At his gray gaze that surrounded her in warmth and comfort and everything that she'd never thought she'd wanted. "Icing?"

He kissed her nose. Then her cheeks. Then her lips. His kiss was chaste. Lingering. Loving.

If she hadn't already been falling for him, she would have now just from the sweetness of his kiss. It didn't shake her to her core, she realized. It filled her to her core.

"But I live at Angel River."

"Or you could live with me."

She looked beyond him at the living room. "Here?"

"Here. Anywhere." He cupped her cheek. "But maybe on a particular meadow that gets covered in wildflowers every June."

Her heart skipped a beat and the flood in her eyes overflowed.

"It really doesn't matter where a home is as long as it's where we both want to be. You know I want to be with you. And I'm pretty sure you want to be with me. But you gotta admit it, sweetheart. You just have to say the words. And I'm yours."

When something seems too good to be true...

She sniffed. "Rory is going to love you."

He gave a half laugh. "Not really the answer I'm after here."

"What you're after is my heart. A heart that you trust."

His eyes suddenly gleamed. "That's the idea. So?

What do you think? A farmhouse on a meadow? Pretty sure you've got a lock on a job up on the mountain if you just say the word."

"Angel's Flight," she said huskily.

"What?"

She smiled and swiped her cheek. "That's the name April and Jed finally chose for the lodge. Angel's Flight."

"It's perfect. But you still haven't answered me, Megan, and I gotta tell you, my patience is about ready to run out."

She ran her fingers through his thick dark hair and stared into his soft gray eyes. Nick Ventura. Whose heart was a carrot that she could no longer deny.

She pressed a soft kiss to his lips, then twisted away from his embrace.

"Megan—"

She went over to the front door and pushed it closed. Flipped the lock.

Then she turned back to him. "You're mine," she said and took his hand in hers. She kissed his palm and pressed it to her heart and then the swell of their child. "And we are yours."

Epilogue

The next day dawned bright and clear and Megan tried hard not to feel self-conscious as she and Nick arrived at the library grand opening where a large crowd had already gathered.

It wasn't so much the fact that she and Nick were holding hands as he led her to the front row of white chairs that had been marked off as reserved, as the dress. The same one from the night before. She couldn't stop twitching at it as they hurried to their spots.

"Relax," Nick told her for at least the third time since they'd left his condo. "You look beautiful in that dress." He sat in the seat next to her and slid his arm around her shoulder. "In fact, I'm hard-pressed to know whether I like your butt in jeans better than

I like your ankles in a dress. Pretty much, I'd rather we ditch this thing, go back to bed and make our own July Fourth fireworks."

"Keep your voice down," she said with a welcome bit of familiar tartness. She was still Megan, after all. Just a richer version thanks to the man beside her. Staying in bed as long as they had was the reason they'd been nearly late. "You're due this celebration, too, remember."

He leaned close, sliding his palm across her belly. "There are other things *due* that interest me more."

She couldn't help melting inside a little and threaded her fingers through his. "Delia's here," she murmured, watching the woman accompany Vivian and several other people—including Rory and Gage—to the front of the library where the mayor stood alongside the blue ribbon stretched across the entrance. Delia wore huge dark glasses and seemed to be keeping her attention on her grandmother, who was holding oversize gold scissors to cut the ribbon.

Nick grunted slightly.

"She didn't have to tell me the truth," Megan pointed out. She'd already told him how Delia had shown up at the motel when Megan had been throwing her stuff into her suitcases, intent on escape. "It wasn't easy for her."

"When you and I are rocking on our front porch watching the grandkids play, I'll think about letting her off the hook."

Megan's eyes were suddenly misty. She lost interest in the ceremonial activity taking place in front of them and focused only on him. "We haven't even had this baby yet and you're already imagining grand-kids?"

"Imagining is where amazing things start, re-member?" He lifted their linked hands and kissed her palm. "Close your eyes and tell me what you see."

But she didn't need to close her eyes. She stared, instead, into his. And saw everything she needed.

"I see you." She kissed his palm in turn. "That'll do for a start…"

* * * * *

Don't miss it as
Return to the Double-C
continues with
A Rancher's Touch
by New York Times *bestselling author*
Allison Leigh.

Available October 2021
from Harlequin Special Edition.

**WE HOPE YOU ENJOYED
THIS BOOK FROM**

HARLEQUIN

**SPECIAL
EDITION**

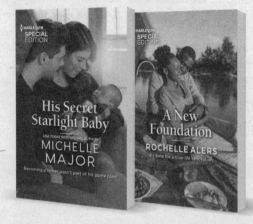

Believe in love. Overcome obstacles. Find happiness.

Relate to finding comfort and strength in the
support of loved ones and enjoy the journey
no matter what life throws your way.

6 NEW BOOKS AVAILABLE EVERY MONTH!

HSEHALO2021

HARLEQUIN

*Uplifting or passionate,
heartfelt or thrilling—
Harlequin has your
happily-ever-after.*

With a wide range of romance series that each
offer new books every month, you are sure to
find the satisfying escape you deserve.

**Look for all Harlequin series
new releases on the
last Tuesday of each month
in stores and online!**

Harlequin.com

HONSALE0521

COMING NEXT MONTH FROM

♦ HARLEQUIN
SPECIAL EDITION

#2857 THE MOST ELIGIBLE COWBOY
Montana Mavericks: The Real Cowboys of Bronco Heights
by Melissa Senate
Brandon Taylor has zero interest in tying the knot—until his unexpected fling with ex-girlfriend Cassidy Ware. Now she's pregnant—but Cassidy is not jumping at his practical proposal. She remembers their high school romance all too well, and she won't wed without proof that Brandon 2.0 can be the *real* husband she longs for.

#2858 THE LATE BLOOMER'S ROAD TO LOVE
Matchmaking Mamas • by Marie Ferrarella
When other girls her age were dating and finding love, Rachel Fenelli was keeping the family restaurant going after her father's heart attack. Now she's on the verge of starting the life she should have started years ago. Enter Wyatt Watson, the only physical therapist her stubborn dad will tolerate. But little does Rachel know that her dad has an ulterior—matchmaking?—motive!

#2859 THE PUPPY PROBLEM
Paradise Pets • by Katie Meyer
There's nothing single mom Megan Palmer wouldn't do to help her son, Owen. So when his school tries to keep his autism service dog out of the classroom, Megan goes straight to the principal's office—and meets Luke Wright. He's impressed by her, and the more they work together, the more he hopes to win her over...

#2860 A DELICIOUS DILEMMA
by Sera Taíno
Val Navarro knew she shouldn't go dancing right after a bad breakup and she definitely shouldn't be thinking the handsome, sensitive stranger she meets could be more than a rebound. Especially after she finds out his father's company could shut down her Puerto Rican restaurant and unravel her tight-knit neighborhood. Is following her heart a recipe for disaster?

#2861 LAST-CHANCE MARRIAGE RESCUE
Top Dog Dude Ranch • by Catherine Mann
Nina and Douglas Archer are on the verge of divorce, but they're both determined to keep it together for one last family vacation, planned by their ten-year-old twins. And when they do, they're surprised to find themselves giving in to the romance of it all. Still, Nina knows she needs an emotionally available husband. Will a once-in-a-lifetime trip show them the way back to each other?

#2862 THE FAMILY SHE DIDN'T EXPECT
The Culhanes of Cedar River • by Helen Lacey
Marnie Jackson has one mission: to discover her roots in Cedar River. She's determined to fulfill her mother's dying wish, but her sexy landlord and his charming daughters turn out to be a surprising distraction from her goal. Widower Joss Culhane has been focusing on work, his kids and his own family drama. Why risk opening his heart to another woman who might leave them?

YOU CAN FIND MORE INFORMATION ON UPCOMING HARLEQUIN TITLES, FREE EXCERPTS AND MORE AT HARLEQUIN.COM.

HSECNM0821

SPECIAL EXCERPT FROM

⟨H⟩ HARLEQUIN
SPECIAL EDITION

*When Val Navarro meets Philip Wagner, she believes
she's met the man of her dreams, until she discovers
that his father's company is responsible for the
changes that could shut down her Puerto Rican
restaurant and unravel her tight-knit neighborhood.
When Philip takes over negotiations, Val wants to
believe he has good intentions. But is following her
heart a recipe for disaster?*

Read on for a sneak peek at
A Delicious Dilemma
by Sera Taíno!

She returned with the pot of melted chocolate and poured
the now-cooled liquid into a cup, handing it to him. Val
fussing over him made him feel positively giddy. He raised
the cup and took a sip. Chocolate and nutmeg melted on his
tongue, sending a surge of pleasure through him.

"Puerto Rican hot chocolate," she said, taking her seat
again. "Maybe the sugar will perk you up."

"You're worried about me falling asleep at the wheel."

"This is how I'm made. I'm a worrier."

His eyes flickered to her strong hands, admiring the signs
of use, and he wondered at what other things she created
with them. "No one's worried about me in a very long time."

He was learning to read her, so he was ready for her
zinger. "In my family, worrying is an Olympic sport, so
if you ever need someone to worry about you, feel free to
borrow any of us."

He smiled into his cup. "I appreciate the offer."

She settled onto the stool, shuffling her feet into and out of her Crocs. "I wasn't really looking for anything tonight."

"Neither was I. But here we are."

Her eyes flicked away again, a habit he was beginning to understand was a nervous reaction, as if she might find the answer to her confusion somewhere in her environment. "That breakup I told you about? That was the last time I've been with anyone."

"Same. It's been a while for me, too." Maybe too long, if his complete lack of confidence right now was any indication.

"Just managing expectations." She poked at her cake, swirling the fork in the fragrant cream. "I'm really not up for anything serious."

"That's fair."

She took a bite, chewing slowly, the gears of her mind visibly working. He didn't rush her, and his patience was rewarded when, after a full minute, she said, "Okay. Next Saturday. I don't work Sundays."

"What if I can't wait until next Saturday?"

"It's like that?" she whispered.

"It's like that," he answered, and she was suddenly so close that if he leaned forward, it would be impossibly easy to kiss her. And he wanted to kiss her badly; the wanting burned hot in his chest. But he couldn't. It would be a lie.

Don't miss
A Delicious Dilemma *by Sera Taíno,*
available September 2021 wherever
Harlequin Special Edition books and ebooks are sold.

Harlequin.com

Copyright © 2021 by Sera Taíno

HSEEXP0821R

Get 4 FREE REWARDS!

We'll send you 2 FREE Books plus 2 FREE Mystery Gifts.

Harlequin Special Edition books relate to finding comfort and strength in the support of loved ones and enjoying the journey no matter what life throws your way.

FREE Value Over **$20**

YES! Please send me 2 FREE Harlequin Special Edition novels and my 2 FREE gifts (gifts are worth about $10 retail). After receiving them, if I don't wish to receive any more books, I can return the shipping statement marked "cancel." If I don't cancel, I will receive 6 brand-new novels every month and be billed just $4.99 per book in the U.S. or $5.74 per book in Canada. That's a savings of at least 12% off the cover price! It's quite a bargain! Shipping and handling is just 50¢ per book in the U.S. and $1.25 per book in Canada.* I understand that accepting the 2 free books and gifts places me under no obligation to buy anything. I can always return a shipment and cancel at any time. The free books and gifts are mine to keep no matter what I decide.

235/335 HDN GNMP

Name (please print)

Address   Apt. #

City   State/Province   Zip/Postal Code

Email: Please check this box ☐ if you would like to receive newsletters and promotional emails from Harlequin Enterprises ULC and its affiliates. You can unsubscribe anytime.

Mail to the **Harlequin Reader Service:**
IN U.S.A.: P.O. Box 1341, Buffalo, NY 14240-8531
IN CANADA: P.O. Box 603, Fort Erie, Ontario L2A 5X3

Want to try 2 free books from another series! Call 1-800-873-8635 or visit www.ReaderService.com.

---

*Terms and prices subject to change without notice. Prices do not include sales taxes, which will be charged (if applicable) based on your state or country of residence. Canadian residents will be charged applicable taxes. Offer not valid in Quebec. This offer is limited to one order per household. Books received may not be as shown. Not valid for current subscribers to Harlequin Special Edition books. All orders subject to approval. Credit or debit balances in a customer's account(s) may be offset by any other outstanding balance owed by or to the customer. Please allow 4 to 6 weeks for delivery. Offer available while quantities last.

Your Privacy—Your information is being collected by Harlequin Enterprises ULC, operating as Harlequin Reader Service. For a complete summary of the information we collect, how we use this information and to whom it is disclosed, please visit our privacy notice located at corporate.harlequin.com/privacy-notice. From time to time we may also exchange your personal information with reputable third parties. If you wish to opt out of this sharing of your personal information, please visit readerservice.com/consumerchoice or call 1-800-873-8635. **Notice to California Residents**—Under California law, you have specific rights to control and access your data. For more information on these rights and how to exercise them, visit corporate.harlequin.com/california-privacy.

HSE21R

Don't miss the fourth book in the touching and romantic Rendezvous Falls series from

JO McNALLY

It's never too late for a second chance...

"Sure to please readers of contemporary romance."
—*New York Journal of Books* on *Barefoot on a Starlit Night*

Order your copy today!

HQNBooks.com

PHJMBPA0721R